THE BELLS

by
d.ennis

Copyright © 2006 by d.ennis

All rights reserved.

*No part of this book shall be reproduced or transmitted
in any form or by any means: electronic, mechanical, magnetic or
photographic, including photocopying, recording
or by any information storage and retrieval system
without prior written permission of the author.
No patent liability is assumed with respect to the use of
the information contained herein.
Although every precaution has been taken in the preparation of this book,
the author assumes no liability for errors or omissions.
Neither is any liability assumed for damages resulting
from the use of the information contained herein.*

*This is a work of fiction. Names, characters, places, and incidents
either are the product of imagination or are used fictitiously.
Any resemblance to actual events, locales or persons, living or dead,
is entirely coincidental.*

ISBN 0-7414-3681-7

Printed in the United States of America

Third Edition, November 2007

The Bell Cascade and associated logos
are the property of Cast In Bronze

Foreword

Bells have always been a part of my life. I started playing the carillon as a young man, but was never exactly sure why. A few years later the carillon would play a role in saving my life, ring for my wedding, and lure me to France to enroll in the French Carillon School. I returned to the United States and took a position selling and installing bells and carillons. But when my musical goals were not being realized, I became so frustrated and depressed that I vowed never to play the carillon again.

Some years later, the bells called me back again. My first carillon teacher died, and I was asked to play the carillon for his funeral. I was ashamed that it was the death of someone close to me that brought me back to the carillon. I succeeded him as carillonneur of the Washington Memorial Chapel in Valley Forge, Pennsylvania and resolved that this was the sole reason for my playing the carillon all these years.

However, more bells came to me in the form of a transportable carillon provided by a benevolent stranger. I created Cast in Bronze, the only musical act in the world that features a carillon combined with other musical instruments. Perhaps *that* is the reason I have played the carillon all these years.

But, things are never as they first appear. I thought I was in control of the bells, but I have learned that the bells are in control of me. I cannot perform without them and they cannot sing to the listener without me. I have lost my identity to the bells and we have become one. I am convinced that they make all the decisions now, and I am just along for the ride.

I have been fairly content these last few years, but the bells are becoming restless and I can actually hear them talking to me once again: "It is time for a book to be written about the carillon. You are going to ask your life-long friend, Dennis Coleman, to write it. Then, this story is going to be transformed into a theatrical production that will feature the carillon on stage for the first time." Dennis didn't have any reason to say yes, but he did.

The bells know you will like this story, for it is about life, love, hope and yes…about them… **The Bells.**

Frank DellaPenna

THE BELLS

In my life, I have wondered these things, more than all others:

-Are we meant to discover whom we were meant to be?
Or
-Are we meant to dream, and to create that which we want to be?

I have learned that whichever we choose, we will need to have faith, we will need to believe in others, and we will need courage. We will need to accept some things and reject others.

And there is so much that I never knew.

"My name is Jacqueline. It is the year 1829. My home is in France, in the town of Douai. In Douai, we are known for the bells that have come and gone, and come again to our town hall. I have seen the joy that they have given, the despair that we have felt from the loss of them, and the magic that they have created.

The bells came here centuries ago. Some say that it was the year 1391, but who can know? They are as much a part of our town as the sea is to a seaport. In my lifetime, I have seen the bells taken down cruelly and I have seen them raised again, as if the hopes and dreams of the people of Douai were being raised with them.

The raising of the bells is a dramatic work. Before I saw it happening myself, I often wondered how such things would rise from the ore of the earth to their home in the tower. I dreamed of it as a child. When I closed my eyes, it was as if they elevated themselves to their place far above us all. I could almost see them rising, as if on angels' wings. Once in place, they would be there for all of the ages. As a young girl, I always felt that when the bells were silent in the tower, they were watching over us.

But, such are the dreams of children. Bells are cast with sweat and toil. We make them, put them in their cradled homes, and set them to work for us.

But, I also know that magic happens when people believe in each other. I know that mysteries unfold when people reach beyond themselves in faith, reach to the extent of their mortal means, and still hope for more. I have learned that destinies are claimed or denied when we take the time to listen, as if we are listening for that still, small voice that is great within us.

In my lifetime, I have listened and sometimes tried, without success, to ignore my destiny. On some occasions, it whispered like the mellow jingle of a sleigh bell. Other times, it was as if I were standing in the middle of the bell tower, surrounded by the pealing of every one of the thirty-five bells.

The bells have come to mean something precious to me, not only by their tones, but also in the way that they symbolize our lives. To me, the bells are like our individual gifts. They will sit there dormantly, until we decide to swing them into work. A still bell makes no music. I have learned if I move my gifts and my hopes and my dreams into action that wondrous things can happen.

Most importantly, I have learned that if I can swing my own bell into chiming and have faith that all of the others bells will do the same, the world becomes a beautiful song.

Here is my story: it begins in the middle. The bells that ruled the tower for centuries had been absent for decades, removed by people who sought to rule over us. After thirty long years, they were finally being restored to our village."

The bells are lifted up again...

As the people in the town manned the many ropes and struggled to raise the bells up to their home at the top of the tower, there seemed to be a hesitancy to fully rejoice in this long-awaited, much-discussed and often-argued act.

Surely, there was no one from the town that was not present at the square on this day for this event. Certainly, no one would miss the historic event of seeing the bells' rise to the top of the tower.

Yes, they were all there: the young and the old, the many who had dreamed of this day, and the few who dreaded it. Those who were largely indifferent were there for the spectacle and some were there to watch the others. Some came to sell their wares or food, knowing that the day would be like market day. Some came to laugh or gossip. Others came to eat or sip wine in the lazy sun that drooped over the heart of town at midday.

The Mayor addresses the town…

"As your Mayor, I am honored to dedicate these bells to our use, for the common good, and to the glory of God almighty. It is a grand day indeed. After thirty long years of having a silent bell tower, Douai will again be known as 'The Town of the Bells'.

In two days, the bells will play for us at Christmas, just as they have done in Douai for countless generations. Father Alphonse will now lead us in the blessing."

The Priest spoke out, from high above them, standing in the bell tower:

"Dear people of Douai: I have washed these bells with holy water, anointed the outside of them with oil for the sick, and anointed the inside of them with chrism. The incense is burning around each of them now.

Let us pray:

We praise You, Lord, Father all holy.
To a world wounded and divided by sin,
You sent Your only Son. He gave His life for His sheep,
to gather them into one fold
and to guide and feed them as their one shepherd.
May Your people hasten to Your church
when they hear the call of these bells.
May they persevere
in the teaching of the apostles,
in steadfast fellowship, in unceasing prayer
and in the breaking of the bread.
May they remain ever one in mind and heart
to the glory of Your name.
Grant this through Christ our Lord. Amen."

The Mayor continued:

"For centuries, the bells called us to work and to worship. They would ring to call us from the field and to signal market day. They would chime at weddings and toll for our loved ones that have passed on.

Although villains once took the bells from us, they were restored to us by faith. When our bell tower became silent, the bells never stopped ringing in the heart of our sister, Jacqueline." At this, there was polite and scattered applause. "On behalf of the entire town, I thank you for always believing and helping us to believe."

The bells of Douai...

Indeed, they were all there on this day, joined again after so long by the very things that once defined them as a town: the bells. The bells of Douai were home once again.

In the long history of the town, the people of Douai defined the eras according to the life of the bells. There was the time when the bells were there, safely in place for one generation after another. They had been there for so long, that *how* they got there had become the subject of many a story of romance or worship or intrigue. The folklore of the bells made Douai a town.

Some said that they knew each individual bell by its voice; some had names for each of the bells. Others thought that one individual bell pealed only for them. Most believed that each bell, like each of them, had a soul of its own and a home in Douai.

In those days, the bells had many tasks to complete. On some occasions, they were the bells of time, the bells of alarm, or the bells that called people to worship. The music cascaded down in the midst of them, over their heads and through them, off and over the hills to the clouds, and back again.

And, as always, the bells would play throughout the twelve days of Christmas, chiming the carols of that blessed season.

The darkest time was when Douai was occupied and the bells were taken away. An army of foreigners treated the beloved bells with such disdain that it was a horror just for the townspeople to know that strangers were even *touching* them.

When the soldiers lowered the largest of the bells down into the waiting wagons, the townspeople were shocked and many cried as the mules pulled the bells away from the square. They smiled secretly when the great weight of a bell caused a wagon's wheel to surrender under the load and shatter. They all felt as though this particular bell was doing its best to stay at its home with them.

When the smaller bells were thrown from the top of the tower to shatter at the foot of the town hall, it seemed as if the townspeople were watching their own children being cast headlong to their deaths. This particular spectacle was too much to watch for many of them, and so they hurried away.

It was hard to believe that even the soldiers of an enemy could be such barbarians.

Those who were there to witness this destruction told and retold the others of the carnage of the bells. With each retelling, the anger multiplied within them. The soldiers, who had treated the soul of the town with such disdain and indifference, never knew that they had planted, by that one act, the seeds of hatred that would one day undo them all.

This hatred was seared into each of the people of the town. The distant and constant smoke finally revealed to them that their bronze bells had been forced, in an act almost like a wicked alchemy, to surrender their shape, resonance and spirit. It went beyond belief. The soldiers had melted down the bells to be reshaped into cannons. The townspeople knew these weapons would be used to kill their own.

A few, who were there as the smaller bells shattered at their feet, managed to slip a small piece of the bells into the grips of their hands. These few chunks became relics, equal to the bone of any saint, to the good people of Douai.

The years that followed could have been called: *the time without the bells*. But they never were. From the time of the destruction of the bells until that day when these new bells found homes in the yokes of the elder bells, the people refused to speak of the bells in the present.

For those long thirty years, the bells were spoken of in the future tense: *when the bells return*...or *when we have the bells again*...it was always some version of *the bells are coming*.

And, it was not until their future hopes became the reality of the present that they could say: *the bells are here*. Indeed, the bells had returned. And there was no one to play them.

When the last of the bells was hoisted into place and cradled into the spot that would become its home, the sweating men and the watching crowd were all caught up in the feeling that, after more than thirty years, they had *finally* replaced the bells.

It was as if the people had restored their own personal dignity. It was as if all of the family was assembled around the table at Christmas.

So much time and energy and sweat and toil had been put into this effort. The realization that it was finally done caused everyone to stare up at the tower. After a time, the chatter subsided and the square was quiet. Oh, so quiet.

It seemed as though they all settled on the same reality, as if they were of one mind. They were all waiting for the bells to play.

Nervously, townspeople shifted their weight from one foot to another. They looked heavenward toward the bells, and then looked at each other. Some took to staring at their feet. They began to murmur, and the murmuring began to build into a slow and raucous mix of bewilderment and anger.

The Maestro volunteers...

The scene that followed was almost comical as it unfolded:

Vincent had been the town carillonneur for more than fifty years. Besides his pompous carriage, the fact that he acted like the bells belonged to him alone caused the town to ridicule him behind his back by referring to him as "The Maestro." He had been absent from the square for more than a year, as his health was failing. The absence of the bells gave him no reason to appear. He had been living in the care of his daughter, who believed that the news of the bells finally being lifted up again would provide him comfort in his dying days.

No one expected him to appear, but there he was on the square, wearing the cape that he believed gave him an air of aristocracy.

Slowly, he shuffled up to Jacqueline and with all of the strength that his ancient voice could muster, said: "*I* shall play the bells."

It was painful for them to watch his slow progress up the steps of the town hall. When he reached the front door, a man joined him and took his arm, knowing that the many steps to the bells would be a nearly impossible trip for him.

Vincent shook the man's arm off of his own with a growl and turned to look at the assembled crowd. He thought of them as his own audience, and he was aware of those who were grumbling with impatience.

Vincent had lived his entire life as though he was the lead actor in a play that cast the rest of the townspeople as an adoring multitude. He played this part so well that he had convinced himself long ago that it was true. Although Vincent was unable to admit it, he suspected it was the bells that held the hearts of Douai, and not him.

If Vincent had exalted the bells rather than himself, he would have received the love and respect that he desired so greatly. Some believed that the bells refused to fully cooperate when Vincent played them, as if they held a grudge against him. The bells obeyed his command, as a slave obeys a master: the work would be done, but without joy.

When a few voices finally expressed impatience, Vincent responded: "I have waited thirty long years for my bells to return. Just as they now silently wait for me, you should wait in silence also. Wait now, until I am inspired."

At first, the crowd was quiet. Then, the grumbling began anew, followed by a few catcalls. When Vincent sensed that they would wait no more, he twirled his cape majestically and passed through the door. They waited a small eternity for him to complete the trip. And then, the bells rang…simply and plaintively.

When the piece was completed, there was polite applause and a few cheers, followed by thorough silence. In respect, the townspeople waited for Vincent to make his descent.

When at last the door to the town hall opened, he stood and faced them all, with something of a contorted look on his face. He raised his arms slowly above his head, attempting a look of majesty. The assembled silence was unnerving. When a woman finally spoke, it seemed to awaken them all: "What happened to the last note of the song?"

When she spoke, it seemed as if she was speaking for them all. Other voices repeated the same question. Some wondered aloud if the aged Maestro was as aware of the missing note as they were.

Still others were more charitable, saying that they could not expect the old man to be perfect, as thirty years had passed since he last played the bells.

Vincent heard it all. When they finally quieted, he spoke to them. His face held the same odd expression, and his hands had remained in the air. When he spoke, he began pumping them with fists of rage.

"My instrument is incomplete and unacceptable! The bell founder has made fools of all of you and has attempted to discredit me!"

Vincent's eyes scanned the crowd until they rested on Paul, the bell founder, who had worked without payment or any need for gratitude, to recast the bells of Douai.

As Vincent grabbed his cane, he pointed it maliciously toward Paul, and began to approach him. The crowd moved to open a pathway between the two men, and Vincent moved with surprising speed for a man of so many years, for the first two steps. On the third step, which brought him within a few feet of the puzzled bell founder, he threw down the cane. On the fourth step he faltered, then fell. There was no fifth step.

Vincent lay there, dead to the world, in the shadow of the bells and at the feet of Paul, the bell founder. The shriek from his daughter pierced the air as she ran to him.

At first, she screamed, "Father! Father!" This was quickly followed by the words, "This is *your* fault!" which were directed unmistakably toward Paul.

Grabbing her father's cane, she began swinging it toward Paul, in the way that everyone knew Vincent had intended. A man of the village encircled the woman in his considerable arms and held her until the rage yielded into tears. As she began to cry, she let the cane fall to the ground. Amidst the woman's sobs, the man spoke to Paul:

"This is *your* fault, bell founder! We expected so much when you found your way to our village and promised to restore our bells, asking nothing in return. Nevertheless, you have cheated us, sir. Where is the last bell?"

Several from the crowd asked, "Why did you not make the last bell?"

Paul did not respond immediately. As he stood in the crowd of strangers, he wished that he had left Douai as soon as he had completed his work, as he had wanted to. He was looking around the crowd for Jacqueline, to remind her that he had stayed for the festivities of the day only at her request.

Paul thought of the passage of time and events that had brought him to this moment. He took in the looks directed toward him from the crowd and could feel all of their anger and disapproval.

His own anger began to rise, and he thought of how terribly ungrateful they were. At the same moment, he considered that all he had hoped to gain by recasting these bells was lost.

As he thought of all these things, another voice asked, in a manner that was more accusing than inquiring: "Why did you not make the last bell?"

He responded with immediacy, and bellowed his answer and clearly addressed them all: "That was *all* of the metal that I had. There was not enough metal to make your last bell! Perhaps, you should consider all of those bells that I *did* make."

Like many words that are spoken with a misunderstanding at their foundation, these words incited the crowd all the more.

"Since he does not seem to care about our missing bell, I say we hang him in its place!"

"Hang the bell founder!" began to be repeated by several others, until it became a chant voiced by many.

Others began to blame Jacqueline:

"This is all Jacqueline's fault! She is the one that brought him to us. She must have known and thought that she could fool all of us, *and* Vincent."

Vincent's daughter, hearing her father's name, said, "This is all Jacqueline's fault. She brought false hope to my father, and now he is dead because of *her*!"

Silence came only when two men wrapped Vincent in his beloved cape and lifted him to carry his corpse from the square. His daughter fell in line behind them. For the moment, the townspeople forgot all of the eccentricities of their dead Maestro. The many jokes and imitations that they had made of him over the years were subdued in appropriate reverence for the dead man.

The silence lasted until Vincent, his daughter, and the two pallbearers were out of view. Then, a voice was heard. Its message was clear, and undeniably true. The tone was appropriately melancholic.

"We are missing a bell, and we are missing our Maestro. We were better off with no bells."

Paul looked nervously toward the ground as the words were said. He wondered if the attacks against him would start again. He wondered where the woman was who so longed for the bells.

Others began to talk quietly amongst themselves. Paul heard someone say the words that he was thinking: "Where is Jacqueline?"

Another voice said, "A bell is missing, and without all of the notes, there can be no song."

Fearing that the anger was about to return, the Mayor did his best to call the crowd to silence, although he had no idea what words might satisfy them. Like all of the people of Douai, the Mayor felt disappointed. Just moments ago, the bells had been lifted up again so triumphantly, and yet, still remained silent.

More than the anger and the accusations, the people of Douai shared one common feeling: they were all confused.

It was then that Jacqueline moved through the crowd to stand alongside the Mayor. At first, she said nothing.

The Mayor asked, "How will we cast this last bell, Jacqueline? The bell founder said that there was not enough metal to cast another bell."

"Who is it that will play the bells, Jacqueline?" the people asked. Despite the somber air of the moment, several people laughed nervously. Jacqueline was unperturbed.

No one to play the bells…

A voice finally rose above all of the others, repeating the words that expressed the feelings of the townspeople:

"Bells…we have the bells. But, the bells have no song."

Voices rose, then lowered, and then rose again. They all fell to silence when Jacqueline raised both hands in the air in a way that was far more dramatic than her usual manner. She addressed them all, almost in an exhortation, with these words:

"Have we forgotten everything?"

Jacqueline waited until every pair of eyes was focused on her. She walked in and out amongst them, sometimes staring, sometimes glaring. She walked up to one and said, almost in a whisper, "Have you forgotten?" and then turned and pointed across the crowd in such a way that everyone there knew who her target was, and bellowed, "Have *you* forgotten?"

Jacqueline continued to walk amongst them all, pointing, asking and accusing. Their eyes followed her, their ears intent on her words. She stopped in the middle of them and said:

"I am one of you, yet so few of you know very much about me. I was born in Douai and by God's grace I shall die here. I was eighteen years old when they took the bells from us. On that day, I felt as though I had lost all that I had and all that I am. In time, I would learn that there was far more that I would lose.

My father was born here, as was his father, as was his. My mother always said that the first thing she could remember as a child was the sound of the bells, because they broke the silence.

My father would tell me how the villagers and the farmers would come to this very place when the bells called to them. He would recall the times when he and his young love would sit or lie in the fields and let the music of the bells waft over them. My father used to tell me many things, but that was long ago. When love came into my life, it caused a breach between my father and me that not even time could repair.

In happier times, my mother and father claimed that the bells were the instrument that brought them together."

Jacqueline's mother, Christine, tells her story...

"We were at the square on market day. Pierre was there, going about the family business of selling fruits and vegetables. Pierre always said that it was on that day that he first took full notice of me. Of course, as we were both villagers, we had seen each other many times before, but we had never noticed each other in the way that we did on that day.

It was late in the afternoon and the square was beginning to empty. I was meandering about, carrying a folded cloth filled with tomatoes which was tucked into my apron, as I waited for my mother to complete her shopping and gossiping.

Vincent, whom some referred to as "The Maestro", was playing the bells. The song, although I didn't know it at the time, was called "Hand in Hand". It was the most beautiful music I had ever heard. Pierre always said that the music seemed to carry him from the spot where he stood and across the square to the steps of the town hall. He was approaching the steps, eating an apple, with his eyes up toward the sky. He was watching the clappers of the bells move back and forth, as though he could see the notes as they were being played. I was drawn into the music in the same way, walking toward the steps of the town hall, leaving my mother to gossip with her friends.

We collided completely and entirely into each other, tripping over the first step. Pierre fell directly upon me, his apple landing between us. The tomatoes that I carried were squashed as we sank into a heap together. As we considered what had just happened, he could only laugh, and I could only scream. My screaming caused Pierre to rise quickly to his feet, all the while being punched and pushed by me, as I screamed the word "Oaf!" over and over.

My screaming and his laughing quickly caused my mother to race to us and she began to assist me in hitting Pierre, although she did not know why. She could only read the look on his face, and the fact that her daughter was covered with smashed tomatoes. As soon as my mother was certain that I was not hurt, she insisted that Pierre replace the tomatoes, which he refused to do. We stormed from the square, my mother dragging me by the arm.

As we passed the people, they began to laugh at the sight of me, which hurried my mother's pace all the more. The man who was to become my husband always said that the image of me covered in tomatoes remained lodged in his mind.

It was a few months later, on one of those nights when Vincent would play the bells for us all, that we saw each other again. He was leaning against a wall, and I was seated across the square with my mother and father. I had become a little distracted and was daydreaming when I noticed that it was the song "Hand in Hand" that was being played. It haunted and inspired me then, as it had the first time that I had heard it. Without even considering my actions, I began to walk dreamily toward the foot of the town hall, with the feeling that a steady force was drawing me there somewhat urgently.

When I arrived at the steps, it was as if Pierre was coming to meet me, drawn by the same force. When I saw his face, I felt embarrassed. I know that I blushed. He smiled first, and then I did, and then we began to laugh as we stared intently at each other. Before the laughter subsided, we knew we were in love.

"Hello, Christine," he said.

"Hello, Pierre," I answered, aware that I was nervously staring at my feet.

I can still hear his voice saying my name. It was a far more welcome voice than I had heard on our last meeting.

Pierre worked up the courage to meet my father within a week.

Christine tells the story of her father…

"On the outside, my father was a gruff man, or so it seemed. On the inside, he was even worse. When Pierre came to see him, I was hiding nearby and listening. Being nervous, Pierre quickly made the point with him that he wished to court his daughter. My father did not hesitate in saying, 'No', with great volume. Pierre also did not hesitate in foolishly proclaiming that there was nothing that my father could do or say that would keep him from me…Ah, the unbridled brazenness of youth.

My father stared at my suitor for some time without speaking. I was beginning to fear that Pierre would take back his words. All seemed to be lost when he headed wordlessly for the door. As he reached the door, my father bellowed out the word, 'Christine!' which brought me rushing to the table from the spot where I was hiding.

'Christine, this man says he wishes to court you and that there is nothing that I, your father, can do to stop it!'

He looked into my face for so long that I knew he wanted to know my heart and not my words. After an eternity he said, in a voice that was only somewhat softer, 'By the look on both of you, I think that it is true. There is nothing that I can do to stop him.'

Soon after, we married. Within a year, Jacqueline was born. In time, the bells that brought my husband to me would take our daughter away."

Jacqueline continues briefly...

"So I am here in this world because of the bells. Do you think that this is a coincidence? And you, sir, do you think that the bells have no power over your life?

Let me tell you of Robert. More than forty years ago, Robert came to Douai to escape the sea. He was not fit for a life at sea because his stomach would not endure it. His stomach overruled his heart's desire to spend a life of adventure on the seas. He planned to learn the ways of ships and one day have his own, so that he could amass great riches by moving cargo and goods around the world. He had dreamed of it since he was a child, and he was only a boy of thirteen when he first went to sea. Tell them, Robert. Tell them all how you came to settle in Douai, and the bells came to be your friends."

Robert's story...

"I was green from the moment that the ship left port. Land was still in sight, and I had already lost many pounds from heaving over the side. Most of the sailors only laughed at me and derided me for being unfit for the sea. Some were kinder, and said that soon I would have my sea legs, and I would be fine. Others saw me as bad luck that should be cast overboard to save them all from the calamity that I would surely bring. Ultimately, I found myself below deck and alone.

Every seaman must do his part, but there was very little for a young boy to accomplish when he could not so much as set foot on deck. They tried me at helping in the galley, but old cookie always said that he could smell the bad luck on me, and so I was to have no part in his domain.

I sat below deck, ignoring the rocking of the ocean in the best way that I could. Finally, a deck hand who referred to me as 'useless', threw a pile of old nets at me as I lay on my bunk and said, 'Fix these!' When I asked 'how?' he just told me that with all of the time I had on my hands, I could figure it out. Over time, I did just that.

I learned to take fragments of string and braid them so tightly that the nets seldom tore, regardless of the weight that they had to endure.

I would take apart worn sections of nets that had long ago been set aside as useless, and slowly wind tiny pieces of rope in a special way that made the nets strong, as if they were made of iron.

Still, a seaman who never sees the ocean is a bad omen to some. I received all of the credit for bad weather, illness and slow winds. The captain, who valued my net-making abilities, refused to listen to the wishes of the crew that sought to rid themselves of me. So they conspired to do so in their own way.

I can recall some of what happened. We put ashore at Normandy. We expected to be there a fortnight or less, unloading cargo from India and taking on more to bring to Northern Africa and Spain.

As soon as we put ashore on our very first night in Normandy, I was more than surprised when several of my "friends" implored me to join them. I did so readily, as a young boy can barely resist the temptations to be found in a café.

When I think back upon it, I can recall how they watched me so carefully and continued to encourage me to drink the ale, and then some wine. I drank so much that they were able to put me in the back of a hay wagon, where I slept through a long and bumpy ride. When I awoke, I had no idea that I was in Douai."

"And yet you stayed here?" someone asked.

"It became my home. I had no idea how far I had come from my own home and I had no wish to return to the sea. In the end, the bells made me stay."

"How is that?"

"The bells are heavy indeed. When they first tried pulling them from below, the meager ropes that they had would not carry the weight. I was here in this town for less than a fortnight, without any idea of what I might do, but I carried an odd feeling that I should stay here. I was watching the ropes fail over and over, and knew that I could help. It took many weeks, but by using the ropes and string that they had, and combining the skills that I learned at sea, it was my ropes that carried the bells to their new home."

Jacqueline continues…

"So, the bells gave Robert work in Douai. The bells brought my parents together. And, the bells brought the song of love to me. Unlike my parents, though, the love that the bells brought together, man *was* able to put asunder. In my life, I have sometimes wished that I could curse those bells. I could not.

I am a simple woman, the child of people who work enough to keep themselves alive. People like us, the farmers and the peasants, learn in our earliest days that we are, in some ways, kept alive by those people whose money does not come from toil.

I always knew of the people that live in houses with the long lanes, lined by trees that flower, rather than fruit. These were the people that would come to market in their carriages to buy the items that we would grow or make. They were the people who would sometimes go off in those carriages to distant places, like Paris, or to the harbor where a ship would take them to the places that are only names to people like us. As a young girl, I somehow understood that my place in this world was lower than theirs, and so I learned to defer to them. They treated me and the others in that manner.

That is why it was beyond all surprise and comprehension when, at age seventeen, Henri, the handsome young son of those people who lived in a house that seemed like a castle to me, spoke to me as his equal.

I will admit, I was captivated by him. Henri would come to the square, brought by carriage and footman for his appointment with the Maestro. His family had the means to engage the Maestro so that he would teach Henri to play the bells. This, of course, further elevated the fortune and the status of the Maestro.

Nonetheless, he was able to help Henri to master the bells. And master them he did. The fact that we, the people of the village, could distinctly tell when Henri would be coaxing and seducing the bells with such passion, would in some ways lead to Henri's undoing.

The Maestro played the bells as if he were commanding them to respond to his will. You could feel their response, but the bells seemed reluctant. It was the way in which Henri played, as the years of his apprenticeship passed by, which caused me to know him. I would sit here on the square and listen, as I would sell fruits and vegetables with my parents. Sometimes, I would find myself seeking out a place to be alone so that I could dance, twirling and spinning in my skirts, arms outstretched and face to the heavens. At other times, I simply danced as I walked.

Many times, when Henri would come down the steps from the tower following the Maestro, I would watch him as he walked across the square. Even in those times when the Maestro was deriding him, I would watch him as his beautiful eyes scanned across the square, as if he were searching for someone. When he would see me, he would smile, regardless of whatever scolding he was receiving from the Maestro. I can recall that smile still.

I recall a particular scene in the square, when the Maestro and Henri's parents were discussing Henri's progress with the carillon:

'He plays like a woman, without distinction or command!' the Maestro would bellow. Henri's parents would listen attentively, learning that many, many more hours of the Maestro's valuable time would be required to improve Henri's playing.

Henri understood that it was all just a ruse to further line the Maestro's own pockets with his father's money, so he made no effort to protest. In addition, he was staring at me, a girl who worked in the market a short distance away, with all of his attention.

I recall the day that he first came to me so that he could get to know me. He made no pretense of buying fruits or vegetables. He was bold, yet sweet in his words.

'I am Henri,' he said.

'I know,' I said, 'I am Jacqueline.'

'Jacqueline,' he said, forming my name on his lips for the first time. 'Hello, Jacqueline.'

In the weeks that followed, it was my mother who first noticed Henri's attention toward me. She was keenly aware that I was receiving attention from the son of Jean-Marie DeVille, who carried the title of Count.

I was too young and naïve to see it, but my heart was flushed when she told me of it, for I was already in love with Henri. My mother, in her own way, approved of this. My father, to be sure, did not.

I understood, without explanation, each of my parents' feelings. I would hear my father talk with my mother in low tones regarding Henri's intentions. He used words that were unkind and angry.

Henri would come around to the square, and we would talk endlessly, seated in the shady spots. We would walk outside of the town and into the vineyards, enjoying each other's company. Henri was a few years older than I, but he was decades beyond me in sophistication and knowledge. He told me of the places he had been, and I would listen in fascination.

When he would come to play the bells with the Maestro, I would always listen beyond normal listening. He would tell me a piece that he would play for me. When he did, it was as if we were all there together: the bells, Henri and me.

Often, he would tell stories of the ridiculous pomposity of the Maestro, and we would laugh hysterically. Sometimes, Henri would imitate him, saying:

'You are *not* the master of the bells, as I am. Play them, you fool! Play them!'

As he did so, he would twirl the ends of an imaginary mustache, just as the Maestro did, and our laughter would be uncontrolled. We longed for time away from the curious eye of my mother and the disapproving looks of my father. And so, we plotted to meet in the moonlight. Henri arrived on a horse at the grove. It was a favorite spot of mine as a child, just over the hill from our cottage.

As I snuck quietly past my sleeping parents, I felt both thrilled and scared to be going off to meet my love under the swept arches of a grove, on a night lit majestically by the moon.

As I approached, I saw him there in shadow. He came to me deliberately, and our kiss, the very first, seemed to fill both of our hearts and all of the air that surrounded us.

After a time, we sat on a blanket that he spread out carefully beneath a tree, and we talked of days ahead. His normally confident way of speaking began to erode. I could hear trembling in his voice. His eyes were locked with mine when he blurted out nervously:

'Jacqueline, be my wife!'

At that moment, I had no thought of the class differences that society placed upon us, or the concerns of my father. They were simply nonexistent in the world that occupied my lover and me.

Before the sun rose, we had given ourselves to each other in complete surrender. As we could feel the sun almost breaking the horizon, we made a promise to keep our plans to marry to ourselves, for now. We vowed to speak of it again in two nights, at the same place and time.

Henri was not at the square the next day. I thought little of that, as it was not expected that he would be there daily, and I knew little of his life at the manor. I do recall that my mother asked me repeatedly that day, '*What* has gotten into you?'

I wanted to tell her all, but honored my promise to Henri. *There would be time enough*, I reasoned.

As I awaited our next meeting, I can recall what seemed to be several eternities. I had no idea of the eternities that would follow.

I walked slowly through the night, toward the grove, under a moon that was now on the wane. I saw him there, as before, shadowed in the overhanging trees of the grove.

I quickened my steps as I greeted him with the word, 'Darling!'

I was frightened to see that it was the Count, Henri's father, who stepped from the shadows. I was beyond speechless.

The Count had a reputation as a mild and gentle man, although I had never spoken with him. But like all of the others in and around the town, I knew little of him.

He spoke to me gently, yet firmly: 'My dear girl, Henri has told me of his proposal to you. I am sure you know that this cannot be.'

His words shocked me back into the real world. That world was inhabited not only by Henri and me, but also by my parents, his parents and the townspeople: a world that knew Henri and I were of different circumstances. In that world, I knew that what the Count said would be considered the truth.

'Henri tells me that he loves you, and I believe him. But your love, dear girl, will not be enough. The world will not support your marriage, just as I cannot.'

He pressed a small leather pouch into my hand and walked to the edge of the grove, where a tied horse awaited him. He mounted his horse and rode away, as I remained standing in the same place. I cried until I no longer had tears to shed.

The next few months were dark ones for me, indeed. I can recall now that I walked, as if in a mist, throughout my days. My parents would ask unceasingly what was wrong, and I would not answer. When Henri would come to play the bells, he would not seek me out at the market. When he would see me seated in my usual spot, waiting for him to descend from the tower, he would smile weakly. I took some comfort in the fact that I could see the look of one who was as broken-hearted as I."

The foreigners come to Douai…

"In the next few months, many calamities befell our town. Foreigners had come and occupied Douai. It was said that they even occupied the manor where the Count and Henri lived.

They had removed our bells in preparation for war. Some of the bells were lowered onto wagons pulled by mules. The smaller bells were thrown headlong, crashing onto the square.

It was chaos. Many of us were grabbing at the fragmented pieces of the bells in disbelief. As I fled the town, I nearly ran into Henri without seeing him."

When Jacqueline came to this part of her story, she looked exhausted.

Everyone knew Jacqueline, it seemed, although no one seemed to know very much *about* her. She had a little flower shop on the square, but most times she could be seen selling flowers from the cart that she pushed around.

Jacqueline would visit with everyone she passed, sometimes selling flowers and sometimes continuing the mission that she carried for thirty years…the mission of bringing the bells back to Douai. Some of the younger people were not aware of this.

The quiet, confident, and solitary woman that some referred to as "the flower lady" and others called "the bell lady" walked every day within feet of her own parents. And yet, no recognition passed between them. She would speak occasionally with her mother, but this was always kept secret from her father.

Some people said that Jacqueline talked about the bells to avoid talking about herself. It was surprising to them all that she was telling her life's story to those who were at the square that day.

Jacqueline said, "Enough about me!"

Louis' story...

"What about Louis?" Jacqueline asked as she shook her finger at the people assembled in the square.

"Can you remember Louis? Can you? If not, I will tell you. Louis was as deaf as deaf could be. As a child, the other children treated him cruelly only because of his infirmity.

If you looked at him, you would notice nothing unusual, except for the fact that he was never with the other children of his age when they played. He would stand silently on the side and observe. He was never encouraged to join in.

The worst of the ridicule was saved for when he tried to speak. If Louis could have heard what the children said, his heart would have been broken for sure. When one of the other children did something unusual or extraordinary, Louis would just call out words of excitement or encouragement. But, they were not words that anyone would understand. They were guttural noises that sounded nothing like a word, and they were so loud! Often, he would clap his hands as he did so, which made him all the more amusing to the other children.

Sometimes, one of the children would sneak up behind him and clap his hands as loudly as possible. Louis, deaf as a stone, never even flinched. That is, until he saw all of the other children laughing directly at him, without knowing why. He did his best to conceal his sadness, but it was there nonetheless.

But, there was something that Louis *could* hear. When the bells would play, somehow it was evident that Louis could hear or perhaps *feel* every note.

I don't know if Louis was jubilant because the bells were playing, or because he could actually hear *something*, but he made no effort to hide his joy. For in that joy, he was no longer the subject of ridicule.

When the bells played, they made their way into Louis' head, and he would dance about, arms in the air, somehow aware of the notes and the rhythm. Often, he would sing, parroting the note of each bell, even before its resonance had diminished and the next note began to fill the air.

Some people said that he must be able to feel the vibrations of the bells. Perhaps that is so, but no one else ever said that *they* could feel anything. For the rest of us, the bells came to us through our ears.

The fact that Louis could not hear meant nothing to the stubborn bells, it seems. They found their way to him through his heart and came out of his mouth, with unexplained and coarse accuracy.

Some would say it was a miracle. Some would try to explain through science how Louis could hear. But, no one would dare to explain how he took on the voice of the bells. I had little trouble understanding. I accepted the magic of the bells, as did Louis."

Jacqueline was motivated now. She could look into the crowd, see their faces, and be reminded of their stories. She called out across the crowd that had assembled around her:

"What about you, soldier? Do you know the bells?"

No one responded as Jacqueline asked these questions. After long moments of silence, a man spoke. He spoke softly at first, and then with more weight and gravity, as his memory took him to a time long ago.

A soldier's story...

He pointed vaguely toward the hills outside of town as he spoke: "When the foreigners came to our town, it was to make it their own. They would camp over there.

They walked in and out amongst us as if we were their chattels. In fear of them, that is what we became: their possessions. I feel shame at the memory that I became a soldier with them. But, I was a boy of sixteen. And, like others, I was told that I would fight with them, or I would perish at their own hand.

They forced me to become one of them. On the day that the bells were taken, I was at the camp, fueling the large fire that they forced us to make.

I watched with sadness and horror as our bells were loaded into the giant cauldrons, as they finally surrendered into a molten mass.

The molten metal was poured into large earthen molds. Some days later, when the metal had cooled, we saw that the bells, those instruments of joy and duty to our town, had been recast into cannons.

The bells were now enslaved as weapons. We placed them into a large circle just outside of town. The foreigners wanted us to believe that when the townspeople came to invade us, the cannons would be our salvation. Little did they know…

They did not come, but the occupation continued. I listened and watched as the foreign soldiers, long in their boredom, became more and more bold in the town. They would swagger about and take what they wanted of the wares on market day. One of them wanted a loaf of bread."

The man stopped his story, thoughtfully. His eyes searched about the square, looking for something that only he understood. Then he called out, "Tell them about the bread, Joseph."

Joseph continues the story…

"As you know, I am the baker, along with my brother, Gabriel. Once, there was another baker. He was our brother, named Emile. Emile was the youngest of us. He was a clown, but not a fool. He was braver than the rest of us in his disdain for the occupying foreigners.

Their General, you see, paid us to make the bread for the troops. We did this in shame, but also in the belief that we had no choice.

Some days, as was happening more and more frequently, the soldiers would come by and demand a loaf. My brother and I would acquiesce, but Emile was not as inclined to do so. He would smile at their demands and pretend he did not understand their language. With greater volume and horrific threats, again they demanded a loaf. Emile would not yield.

On this particular day, several soldiers were surprised as Emile said, 'No bread! We have no bread today!' over and over until one of them finally came behind the tables and reached for a loaf, one of three that sat there.

Emile grabbed it first and stared at the soldier without fear or mercy, eye to eye. The soldier reached for another, but again, Emile was too quick, as he held the two loaves in his arms. And so it was with the third.

I was shaking. Emile stood defiantly, almost daring the foreign soldier to do something. The soldier just stood there, as if he had been called to attention. Emile retreated two steps and threw all three of the loaves into the air simultaneously. Then, to our amazement, he began juggling the three loaves high into the air, laughing, as he said, 'No bread today!' over and over.

He stopped only when the bayonet of the soldier had entered him on one side and left him on the other. My brother died with a look of surprise on his face, but with all three loaves cradled in his arms as he collapsed. In fear, I did nothing but watch the soldiers walk away laughing.

That night, my brother Gabriel and I, foolish and drunk, invaded the camp as the foreign soldiers slept. We torched everything that we could."

At this, Joseph walked away, staring intently at the man that had entreated him to tell his story.

The soldier continues...

"The foreigners were incensed. Early the next morning, we pulled the six cannons into a spot just outside the town gates. The foreigners had a new enemy. I knew that I was about to engage in war with my own village.

We formed a line with the cannons, as the foreign soldiers began rousting the men from the town and farms nearby, all because of Emile's act of foolish bravery. Some were killed, while others escaped. The word went out quickly to those in and around the town. A militia of forty or so men was formed inside the stone barn on the Verdins' farm. The men knew that the only thing they could do was attack.

Five other villagers and I were pressed into service as soldiers with the foreigners. We were stationed at the cannons. The foreigners brought the cannonballs and placed them in triangular heaps alongside each cannon. There were boxes of fuse and powder. The foreigners showed each of us how to make the cannons ready and then retreated just behind us.

We knew that if our fellow villagers attacked, we would either fire into them or be killed from behind by the soldiers. We knew it, each of us, without speaking. It was the time of my greatest fear. I am not ashamed to say that I cried, knowing that I would choose to fire these cannons that had once been bells, into my friends, family, and neighbors. The foreigners were confident about their clever plan to have us kill our own.

When the night came, we were ordered to continue manning the cannons while the soldiers lit fires and ate. Feeling relaxed, they began to drink and tell tales of their bravery and of the apparent cowardice of the villagers. I suppose that there were eighty or so soldiers, all armed. And of course, they had the cannons.

At dawn, the forty village men surprised them as they came screaming toward the line of cannons. They were carrying farm tools and pikes. Though they were still far off, their screams frightened even me.

The soldiers, sleepy and groggy from the night before, shouted us into readiness. As soon as they believed that the villagers were within cannon range, they hollered *'Fire!'* and we lit the fuse. There was a loud explosion: a rumbling and a brief, unusual ringing sound. The cannonball flew impotently, no more than five meters. Another cannonball landed less than an arm's length from the cannon.

The foreigners believed that we had each somehow sabotaged the cannons, so they shoved us out of the way to reload them. The second volley was no better. The third was worse. The fourth time the weapons were fired, one of the cannons exploded, killing two of the foreign soldiers.

The soldiers had occupied themselves with the cannons so completely that the villagers were upon them without warning. They attacked them so viciously, it became clear to me and the others who had been forced to soldier that we could join our own people in the fight.

More than half of the foreigners were killed or knocked down almost immediately, compared to only seven of our villagers. The brave men of Douai would not let up as the foreigners retreated into the forest. We never saw them again. However, we lived in fear of retaliation for many months. Many men were brave that day. I was not one of them."

The man paused in his story. You could see that he was still curious about the events of that day, many years ago.

"No one fully understood what happened to the cannons that day, although some tried to fathom and explain it. What I know is this: even though I had surrendered to the belief that I had to serve in war with the foreigners, the bells did not.

Some said that the bells refused to fire on their own town. Others said that they refused to become instruments of death rather than joy. Perhaps that is why I heard them ring when they were fired.
The bells saved us that day. It was a miracle!"

Some of the people had heard this story before. Some were there when it happened. Jacqueline enjoyed watching the looks on their faces as they considered the word "miracle." Before speaking, she paused to let them take in what they had heard.

Jacqueline, at just the right moment, continues...

"I was telling you about when the bells were taken: As I said before, some were lowered onto wagons; the smallest of them were thrown onto the square. Many of us were grabbing at the fragmented pieces of the bells in disbelief. As I fled the town, I nearly ran into Henri without seeing him.

Our eyes locked and we were paralyzed. All around us was mayhem. I was breathless as I said to him, 'I must speak to you.' Without hesitation, he took my hand and we ran and ran, knowing that we would end up in our spot in the grove. As we climbed the last hill, I felt that I could run no more, as Henri swept me up into his powerful arms. We proceeded the rest of the way like that in silence. Once, I kissed him gently on the neck, only because I could not resist doing so.

In our spot at the grove, we sat quietly. I was trying to put together the words that I needed to say. Before I could, my beautiful Henri, with tears in his eyes, told me bitterly how his father stubbornly refused to give us his blessing.

I had long since accepted that reality, but Henri could not, simply because he could not see me as a peasant. He said to me, 'You are my heart…'

Taking his hand in mine, I said, 'The world will not allow us love, Henri. It is simply the way of the world. But, there are some things that the world can endure even less.'

In carefully measured and rehearsed words, I told Henri that his love grew within me. I told him how my mother had accepted this, and how my father had sworn revenge on his head. I spoke of how my mother dissuaded him from this and how the occupation of our town forced him to think of other things.

I assured Henri that I never told them that we planned to marry.

'But, if they knew, it might change everything,' was Henri's immediate response.

I told him that in my world, the common world, some realities are unshakeable. I told Henri that my parents insisted on sending me away, and I had finally acquiesced to their wishes. I would go to St. Anne's Convent to have our child, who would remain there in the care of their orphanage.

Henri swore mightily and struck the ground when I told him. I know this to be the truth: if I had asked Henri to run away to distant lands with me that night, he would have instantly agreed.

I also knew he could not complete that plan. I saw and felt all of that in the words and the eyes of the Count.

If Henri were going to take me away, he would have done so already. He had not, and I understood, deep inside of me, that he could not. He was to the manor born, after all.

When he asked, 'When do you go?' I told him, 'In two days' time.' The reality and the finality seemed to strike him in an odd way. After long consideration, he said, 'I have nothing to give to my own child.'

We stood and prepared to leave each other in silence. I knew that I would have to take the first steps. I walked away, now fully resigned to my own future, my head down, watching my feet cross the ground. It was a surprise to feel his hand on my shoulder. 'Give this to our child,' he said. In his outstretched palm, he held a shard of a fractured bell. In the moon's glow, we discovered together that this small fragment, broken into the shape of an oval, included a raised letter that had once been part of a word, now unknown to us. In the center of the bronze fragment, was the letter " t ". To me, it looked more like a cross. I encircled my fingers around it as Henri kissed me goodbye. I turned from him, somehow believing that I should disguise my tears. It was the last time that I was to see Henri, the handsome young nobleman, whose heart was made for the music of the bells."

When Jacqueline told her story, she made no opportunity for anyone to ask questions. It was clear that this woman was willing to share her darkest times and her nearly fanatical belief in the magic of the bells.

Jacqueline continues her story about her time at the convent...

"I lived quietly among the Sisters. To my relief, they made no inquisition or judgment regarding my condition. They gave me work to do as a washerwoman that I was grateful to have to pass the days and the months. When the time came for our child to enter this world, I cried, knowing he would be alone.

He was a fine boy, the son of his father in looks. He was my child in the way that he seemed to accept his destiny.

The Sisters told me that I could nurse him for seven days only. But beyond that, I would be stating my wish to raise him on my own, away from the convent. I followed their command, as I had accepted that I had no choice but to leave my beautiful son behind to be raised at the convent.

On the seventh evening, I kissed him and placed inside his blanket the small piece of bronze that had a bell as its heritage. Until that time, I referred to him only as "baby." I feared that naming him would bring me too close to him to let him go.

As I was slipping the shard of bell, which was the only worldly thing that I could offer, inside the blanket, I recalled his father's words: 'Give this to our child.' At that moment, I named him Marc, and kissed his cheek. I was kissing him goodbye.

In the morning, my father was there with a wagon he had borrowed from a neighboring farm to take me home. We did not speak of my time at the convent on the ride home, or ever again. In truth, my father has refused to speak to me from that day, nearly thirty years ago, until this one."

Henri is despondent...

Henri was overcome by the world. His father had busied himself with bringing a seemingly endless line of young women to him, none of whom gained Henri's attention, much less his favor.

The occupation by the foreigners, and the fact that his heart had been broken by the loss of his bells as well as his lover, had kept Henri in silence and desperation at the manor every day. Sometimes, he would walk about the gardens and the servants would see him sitting on the garden bench. Thinking that he was alone, Henri would play an imaginary carillon as he softly sang the notes. At other times, he could be heard to cry, and he was left alone to do so.

When he left the manor more than a year later, he left on foot, not knowing how long he would be gone, or where he might go. He simply left, and went to the home of Jacqueline and her parents. He decided that he could no longer live without her. He was still practicing the words he would say to Jacqueline's father:

"I will bring her to the manor and make her my wife." Henri was still rehearsing his speech as he approached her cottage.

When he saw her father walking toward him, he was hopeful, yet terrified. The words that he had planned were never delivered. It was the father who spoke first. They were vile words that were accented by the stomping of the pitchfork that he held in his right hand:

"Get away!"

"Sir, I have come for your daughter."

There are not words that could describe the hatred that was in the eyes of the father, or the fear in Henri's heart. Silence filled the space between them.

"You! You of the bells, and the airs of the rich! You who have everything felt that you could take what was mine! You have killed the girl who was my daughter, and now she is dead to me!"

The look of anger grew on the father's face, as he slowly raised the pitchfork, and held it, ready to strike. Henri did not fear it. In fact, he may have welcomed death at that moment. The father's words swallowed him whole.

Pierre was actually pleased when he saw the tears begin to form in Henri's eyes, just before he turned to walk away. The father watched him walk away until he was out of sight. Henri never once turned to look back.

The father returned to the cottage and considered breaking the silence that he had sworn to keep until his death, by telling Christine all that had happened. Instead, he decided to maintain the silence that began when he banned his daughter from his home, immediately on her return from the convent.

On the few occasions when Christine would mention their daughter, always being sure to use her name, Pierre would say, "I have no daughter," and Christine would always respond, "but *I do*!"

The beginning of a long journey for Henri…

A journey began where he was willing to be led, rather than to adventure with purpose or to explore for excitement. His travels led him to a town no more than a two-day journey away, where he remained Henri, but it was never known that he was the son of a Count.

Henri did not plan to go to St. Anne's Convent, but the thought of the place burned in his chest every day. And so, that is where his heart led him, and his feet dutifully followed.

When he arrived, he realized that he had no thought of what exactly he might do, and he was surprised at the lies he told the Sisters without effort or shame.

"I have come seeking a place of enlightenment and knowledge for my young sister. My father has sent me on this task."

The kind Sister inquired about the girl in question. Since Henri had no sister of his own, he spun tales of beauty, grace and humility about a young girl who sought to serve her Lord by serving the poor, orphaned children of the world.

The Sister soon took Henri to the Mother Superior, who explained the existence of those who seek to live a life of secluded devotion.

They toured the buildings and the grounds together, Henri asking questions of the Mother Superior when it seemed appropriate.

"The orphanage, Sister, may I see it? I want to be able to describe it to my father and my sister in detail."

It was not long before they walked long aisles and humble, low-ceilinged rooms of great length and width, filled with rough-hewn wooden tables and small cots. They came into the garden where the children were either outside working in long-rowed gardens, if their age allowed it, or at play.

Henri's heart was betraying his ruse, as the knowledge that the child that he had never seen was living here, loved, but like an unwanted pauper.

The Mother Superior saw Henri as his eyes filled with tears and his breathing labored. "We do all that we can for them…" she said, as her voice trailed. "You sit here and rest to compose yourself for a moment."

Henri did sit for a few moments, then rose and walked to a small, shaded area where the youngest of the children sat or toddled about. When he encountered his young son, it was apparent to each of them, it seemed, that they belonged to each other. Henri stooped to pick up the boy whose black hair curled like his own. He felt the child's stare pierce him.

Being overcome by all of it, he put the child down and returned to the bench. When he regained his composure, he rejoined the Mother Superior. He thanked her for the visit, promising to return with his father.

Outside the convent walls, his pace quickened at a rate inversely proportionate to that of his sinking heart. Until this very moment, Henri, a child of good fortune, had never felt the weight of shame.

It was the shame that carried him to the next village, and shame that he tried to drink away, one bottle of wine after another, at an inn that he encountered along the way.

It was the wine that encouraged him back to the convent, under the cover of darkness. He walked stealthily into the room where he thought his young son would be sleeping. He crept from one tiny bunk to the next, peering into the sleeping eyes of the children. When he came to his own son, he let out a startled gasp at the vision of the boy who lay there in silence. His eyes were wide open and searching around the room, as if he were waiting for his father to arrive.

He stood over the child for a moment, waiting until their eyes were firmly on each other. It seemed as if the boy half smiled a welcome to Henri, which made him smile in return, as he raised him to his chest.

Turning to make escape, Henri saw a small object reflected in the light, hanging from a nail on a leather strap. It seemed to be a small necklace. At the end of the leather was a small oval-shaped piece of bronze metal. Removing it from the wall, he slipped it into his pocket as they left the convent together.

Henri traveled through a forest all night with the child, until he came within sight of a village. They rested there until Henri was awakened by his son's gentle cries of hunger.

Henri walked to the village, following the smells that indicated a nearby patisserie. He procured two croissants, one of which he devoured in two bites, the other he shoved into his pocket.

Leaving town, and the wine beginning to leave his head, Henri began to consider the fullness of what he had done. As he began to recognize that he knew nothing about caring for such a young boy, he also felt as though he was righting a wrong of his own doing. He carried the child clumsily as he walked, tearing off a piece of croissant for him. Marc consumed it immediately and so Henri followed it with another, then another, until it was nearly gone.

As the child drifted to sleep in his arms, Henri began telling him that he would not be left alone again. The child seemed to understand. Henri said to him:

"I am your father. We will be together now, you and I." The boy looked at him, pointed to his own chest, and said, "Marc."

In a few days, Henri, feeling enough distance between where he was and all he knew, chose a certain village for their new home.

He was also confident that he had constructed enough of an imagined past which would be an acceptable explanation for this unusual traveling couple. By nightfall, he had procured a small room and had learned that he was in a place called Dunkerque. When he kissed his son to sleep, he did so with these words:

"Sleep in comfort, young Marc."

And it was in this way that they arrived in a village by the sea.

Henri searches for work in the seaside village...

Of the many things that Henri had not taken the time to consider, the need to support himself quickly became more important than all of the others.

A young man that has been born into privilege can take for granted that life's staples will just appear for him. The coins in his pocket were dwindling quickly. He would need to find work if he was going to continue in a lifestyle that would leave everything of his previous life, including his name, behind.

Arriving in Dunkerque, Henri walked through the village with young Marc toddling slowly with him. Sometimes, to increase his pace, he would lift the boy onto his shoulders. His devotion to his son was complete.

He knew that if his identity was revealed or he returned to his home, there was a chance Marc would be taken from him. After all, Henri could make no legal claim to his son.

He walked rather casually to the docks, where he purchased a small bottle of milk for Marc, and in paying for it, a quick inventory of his remaining coinage reminded him of his need for work. Knowing that he had never worked a single moment in his life gave him no idea of what he might be *able* to do.

It was at that moment that his eye caught the work of two men who were cleaning a huge pile of fish, just recently placed in baskets along their long wooden table. He watched them at work for a while and observed how people were lining up and waiting to purchase a few of the fillets that they were preparing. It looked easy enough, because the men made it look easy.

Henri began to make casual conversation with them. He noticed how quickly they could remove the head and guts of a fish as they continued in conversation with him, seemingly without looking.

"I am new to this town. I am looking for work." Henri said.

"What is your trade?" one of the fish cleaners asked.

"I can work in the fields. I can clean fish," Henri lied without hesitation.

The two men looked at each other, and then nodded to each other. One of the men nodded his head toward an empty spot on the long table. It was scarred with the shallow marks of a thousand knife cuts. Along the side were three knives in a wooden sheath.

"We can use the help," was all that he said, and all that needed to be said.

Henri, foolishly believing that he could actually clean the fish, brought young Marc around to the side of the table and perched him upon an upside-down basket. He stood behind the table, hoping that he could pass himself off as a cleaner of fish.

He stood there for a few moments, knowing that the eyes of the other two men were on him. Thankfully, a man walked up to the table with a long whitefish in his hand that he had removed from a nearby basket. He threw it on the table in front of Henri.

Grateful for the fact that the situation was now defining itself, Henri quickly went to work on the fish. To say that it did not go well would be to say too little. It did, however, provide entertainment for the other two men, who would watch Henri and then look at each other, trying to hide their laughter.

The customer was too fascinated with the struggle to say anything to Henri. He just watched in disbelief as he devastated the carcass of the poor fish.

When Henri had finished, he slid a pile of mangled fish toward the man and looked at him impassively.

The customer smiled and looked over at the other two fish cleaners, who were doing their best to avoid eye contact and therefore burst into laughter.

"I do not need fish for my cat," the man said quietly to Henri. Henri could sense the pity in the man's voice.

"Please, sir, I need this work." As he said this, he motioned with his head toward his young son.

"You are not a cleaner of fish," the man said. It was not posed as a question.

Henri looked around. Just down the dock, he could see a small shop with a variety of wood stacked neatly about and the array of tools that indicated clearly that it was a carpentry shop. Without pause, he said to the man:

"I am new to this village. I have come here with my young son to find work as a carpenter. Until I can, I must find a way to support us. Please, sir." He said this as he looked down at the pile of massacred fish.

The man thought for a moment, and grabbed a new fish from the basket. He swung it by the tail in front of the other two men, who had stopped their work to enjoy the situation.

The fish was quickly cleaned and wrapped inside a broad leaf and handed to the man. Henri watched it all and hung his head down as the man came back to his spot at the long table.

"Come with me, carpenter," the man said.

Henri picked up his son, gave a long look over his shoulder to the two men, as they did their best not to laugh, and followed quickly in step behind the man. He was surprised when the man walked inside the shop that had been the source of Henri's inspiration moments before, and extended his hand with the words, "I am Claude."

"I am Henri, and this is Marc."

"Tell me, Henri, are you a better carpenter than you are at cleaning fish?"

Henri could have said a thousand things, but not one would have been true. The kindness of this man, regardless of how desperate his own situation, forced him to answer with all honesty:

"I have no skill of any kind, sir. I have only the need and desire to care for my son."

There was a long silence between them…and finally, Claude ended it, saying, "I once had a son of my own."

Henri continued to look at his new friend, while looking around at the carpentry shop. Claude smiled and said, "Hand me that board, Henri, the blackish one."

And so, Henri, Marc and Claude began to spend their days at the carpentry shop together. At the beginning, Claude paid Henri just enough to keep him going. But to everyone's surprise, Henri seemed to have a skill with wood, and his gratitude made him an avid and eager student. When they finished a piece of furniture, Henri experienced the joy that comes from being productive for the first time in his life.

Over time, Claude knew that Henri was contributing to his success as well as his happiness. Claude and young Marc became close as well. Claude treated him like a grandson. As the years passed, Marc displayed a gift for working with the wood that bordered on the work of the finest artisans.

Each day at sunset, Henri and Marc would return to their tiny room at the top floor of the Les Gens de Mer Hotel. Each day at sunrise, they would return to work.

As close as Claude and Henri became, the quiet Henri seldom spoke to him about his life before he came to Dunkerque. Claude always wondered what secrets kept this good man so quiet.

Henri remembers his youth…

Henri was devoted to his son. Their days were spent quietly together at the carpentry shop. Henri often wished that he had more to give to Marc.

In his mind, he would often return to Douai and imagine himself aboard the wide bench of the carillon, making the music that lifted his heart. Sometimes, he would pause from his work and his hands would move, slowly and deliberately, mimicking the movements of playing the bells.

In the evenings, on rare occasions, Henri would speak of his boyhood cryptically. He was always careful to protect his own identity for fear that his son could be taken from him. He spoke of a nameless place, saying only that he lived near a beautiful small town. He would tell his son about the bells and the majesty of living near a town that had such a gift to own and to share.

One day when the father and son were walking back to their tiny room, Marc noticed his father was humming softly. His hands were rolled into fists, making pounding moves.

Marc had seen his father do this before, but it was this time that he took notice that a smile always seemed to cover his father's face as he made the pounding gestures.

Finally, he asked him, "What are you thinking, Papa? When you hum like this, you are always so happy."

Immediately, the father stopped and shook his head slightly to remove himself from the trance. Looking at the boy, he considered his words carefully, finally answering with just one word: "Remembering..."

The father would have been happy to leave it at that, but eight-year-old boys are far too inquisitive to be satisfied with an answer of just one word. And so, Marc asked, "What do you remember, Papa?"
He asked with his eyes far more than his words.

They paused there in the road, the father looking in and through the eyes of his son, looking to see if he truly wanted the answer to the question he had asked. It seemed so.

The two walked just a few more strides when a place, grassy and tree-covered, presented itself to them. They sat, and the father told his son about the bells. He gave him a story, but what he shared with him was far greater. To Marc, it was magic.

For an hour, perhaps more, they sat there. The father said more words in that time than he would generally say in a month. Marc was silent throughout. In that time, he saw his father transformed, for as he told the story, he was no longer the quiet carpenter. He was the man in the tower, the carillonneur, the man who played the bells that lifted hearts.

As he told the story, they both could hear the bells ringing with authority and subtlety: pealing, exhorting and suggesting.

As the father told the story, his hands pounded more enthusiastically, and he would stop and sing the notes that his hands demanded. But, the father never told Marc about musical notes, or how the instrument felt, or the long steps to the bells atop the town hall, or the wooden bench.

He told him how he felt when the bells played. Their song floated over his head. Then, their music drifted down and filled his ears and his heart.

It seemed to lift him up to the clouds, then set him gently down again. He described the market days. When the bells began to play, the people would haggle a little less over prices, and the merchants became more agreeable.

He told of how people would be trudging into town, some weighted down by the load of fruit, wine, cheese or vegetables that they hoped to sell. Others were laden with the worries of how to make a few coins go far enough to procure food for their needs. Henri told of the shepherds fighting the sheep to stay on the road as they headed toward the village. When the bells would begin, the loads of the wagons, and the worries of the heart were lightened equally. People stepped more lively, stopped looking down at the road, and lifted their eyes and their countenance.

He told how the sheep even improved their behavior and began to march hurriedly toward the town, unaware that they were walking toward their new owner or their demise. When the bells played, the people laughed and agreed and they fell in love. Disputes were settled and apologies made.

On the nights when they had the festivals, the bells would pour the wine and light the fire and tell the stories and lead the singing. When the bells stopped, the people stayed around the square. No one was anxious to return to their homes until the magic in the air had slowly left them. But, they always left with a promise to return.

On that day, at the grassy spot along the road, the bells played and the magic of them came into the heart of young Marc, just as it was inflamed in the heart of his father.

When the father stopped, he put his hands, fingers encircled, behind his head and laid his head back onto the grass, closing his eyes gently. His son followed exactly, and they lay there wordlessly until finally, Marc asked the most foolish of questions:

"Can you teach me to play them, Papa?"

The father might have answered that it had been years since the foreigners cruelly transformed the bells into an instrument of destruction. He might have said there were no bells anywhere near them where he could teach his son.

As he began to explain these things, he was surprised to hear himself say, "Yes, I can teach you the bells." And so it was.

In the evenings, father and son would sit quietly in their room. A few candles would burn. There would be wine, bread and a bit of cheese and fruit. The father would sometimes drift off to sleep, and the son would make just enough noise to wake him, hoping for company. Sometimes, you could hear distant sounds enter through the window, and at other times you would hear the sounds coming through the walls from the other tenants.

To teach his son, Henri fashioned a crude carillon similar to the practice carillon that he had played in the tower at Douai. Rather than having a hammer strike a metal bar that closely matched the note of a bell, Henri could only fashion silent wooden pegs to represent the keys of the carillon.

At the carpentry shop, he made two levels of wooden dowels, thirty-five in all, into a long board that he would later secure to the wall in his room at the hotel. These would act as the carillon keys.

He had replicated the carillonneur's bench of his youth, in the best way that his memory would allow.

Sliding the bench in front of the keys against the wall, he marked the pedal positions using black pigment. In this way, he created an instrument that was silent to the world, but resonant in his imagination. He hoped that Marc could learn to hear the tone of each bell as he struck each dowel using the side of his fist.

He would place his feet in the correct pedal position, and position his son just behind him near his right shoulder. He never once considered checking to see if Marc was paying attention. There was no need.

The father would play the imaginary bells, just as if they were there before them both. He was careful in how deliberate he was with the position of his hands as he struck the keys.

He would sometimes strike with passionate, hammering strokes. Sometimes, he was more loving and would delicately graze the keys, as one would do to coax a more subtle sound. And with each stroke, he would delicately sing the note that he would have played, if life had not cruelly removed him from his home, and the bells from the tower.

It was this way for years: the father on the bench, and Marc behind his right shoulder several evenings of each week. Sometimes, Marc would request a particular song or melody. When it was presented, he would ask his father to tell him what memories this song brought to him. Henri would seldom answer.

Sometimes, the father would have a new melody in his head, and he would play it on the bells that only the two of them could see and hear.

Henri and his years in Dunkerque…

They had been together in Dunkerque for fifteen years now, but still Henri spoke of a distant place, and the bells, as his home. All of the years that he had spent in Dunkerque were time spent away from Douai. Once, as they were rubbing the varnish into a table that would soon be in the home of a wealthy family, Marc asked his father if he ever thought that he would go home.

Henri immediately stopped and placed the rag on a hook in the wall. He looked out of the shop and toward the sea, seeming to look beyond the horizon, as if he were looking for the answer. The response was long in coming.

As he went back to his work, his eyes still looking beyond the horizon, he said, "It is no longer my home. My home had bells at the top of the town hall that filled the lives of the people of my town.

Once the foreigners tore the bells from the tower, they tore the hearts from the people and from my own chest as well. I could not bear to return there. There are no bells at my home."

The years passed by with little to mark the change, except that very slowly, the father and the son changed positions.

Claude still came to the shop, but Henri would often nap and come later each day. Young Marc, now a master at working with wood, became the journeyman, and his father worked like the apprentice. It was a wordless evolution that came naturally to them.

Then one morning, Henri simply did not rise from his bed. He was gone from this world. At age seventeen, Marc was once again alone.

Marc needed the wisdom and kindness of Claude. He left his father where he lay and went to the shop. *Surely, Claude will know what to do*, he thought to himself.

Marc knew nothing of death. There were times when he and his father had fashioned coffins of fine wood for the wealthy people of the town; he knew of the cemetery, but he knew nothing of death.

When Claude heard the news of Henri's death, he was overcome with grief and had no words to comfort Marc. They shared a cup of tea and memories of Henri, and eventually spoke of what to do next.

Coaxing Marc by the arm, they went to the pile of wood to select the boards that would become Henri's home in perpetuity. They selected only the finest wood for the coffin. That was their work for the day, and the young Marc continued into the evening until it was done. As he worked, his solitary place in the world became more and more clear to him.

These thoughts became deeply saddening to Marc throughout the afternoon and into the evening. It was the first evening in his memory that Marc had spent without the company of his father. As Marc was finishing the coffin, Claude pulled up, seated at the front of the undertaker's wagon.

Alongside him was Philippe, the undertaker of the town. Together, they loaded the labor of love and necessity onto the wagon.

Claude drew Marc close to him and said, "We will take care of your father now." Marc accepted these words without question. For the first time ever, he walked home alone.

Marc did not feel an immediate sense of loss. Mostly, he was doing his best not to consider that he was entirely alone.

He was overcome with grief, nonetheless.
He grieved over the fact that this man had come and gone from the world, with only a handful of things to show for it: a few candles, plates, and metal cups; no books or jewelry of any kind. As he looked about the stark room, Marc collapsed into heaving cries that his father, this gentle, kindly and dutiful man, had made no mark in the world, and left behind no friends or lover or keepsakes.

He cried for himself, knowing that surely this would be his fate also: to live and die in a world without ever making a difference, or without ever making himself known. Marc walked slowly about the little room, touching the things that his father had touched. He was trying to connect with him, but he could not.

In time, the son took the bench from against the wall and put it in the place where his father sat when he played the bells of his memory and imagination. Marc sat down in his father's spot and waited. He waited, as he always did, for his father to tap his shoulder with the small stick that signaled the beginning of the song. Of course, none came. But, he waited just the same.

He wanted to hear his father's voice sing the tone of the bell, as Marc would strike the imaginary key to play the note. Marc smiled briefly when he recalled how his father would strike the stick on his head when he placed his hand on the wrong imaginary key.

He was grinning more broadly when he recalled how his father would sing the note that Marc had struck, to show him the error. He would sing "bah-bah-bah" as he placed his hand on the imagined key, in the place where Marc had struck, and then move Marc's hand to the correct place, and strike it three times more, this time singing "bum-bum-bum" as the correct note.

Marc could nearly feel his father there in the room with him. And then, for the first time, the music came to him, not in the voice of his father, but in a new voice, a voice that he did not know…a voice that he did not recognize as his very own.

The voice was imitating the pealed notes of the bells about the room. Marc began to play them tentatively at first, fully expecting to feel the occasional tap on his head or the "bum-bum-bum" of his father's voice. When it did not come, his playing became more enthusiastic. And ultimately, it was a wild scene of flailing arms and legs that struck the keys as the bells rang and rang as Marc "played" one song after another. He was aware that he had begun to play songs that he had never heard before. But somehow, he knew them.

Hours passed. When Marc finally removed himself from the bench, he walked slowly to his little cot, sat on the edge of it, his hands on his knees. He was exhausted in a delightful way. *Joyous,* he thought, even in the shadow of the loss of his father.

As he began to lean back and swing his legs onto his cot, he stopped suddenly and stood upright beside the bed. He smiled as he walked over and lay on his father's bed. He was surprised at how bumpy and uneven it felt. He felt at once as if he were almost violating some rule by being there. Alternately, he felt as welcome there as he did when, as a child, he lay in that bed with his father on those nights that he was sick or afraid.

He fell asleep quickly and dreamed deeply and with clarity. He dreamed of lonely bells that called him to their service. When he awoke, he had an abiding sense that the world he knew was gone.

Jacqueline makes a life of her own...

Jacqueline remained detached from her parents. Her father, acting in shame and anger, had banned her from his home with the words, "You are dead to me." He had shared the same sentiment with Henri when he had come for Jacqueline, and had never told her of his visit. There were times when Jacqueline and her mother would speak in secret, but each of them feared and obeyed the command of Jacqueline's father.

To care for herself, Jacqueline used the money that was in the leather purse that the Count had given to her. With this money she procured a small shop on the square, which also became her home.

Each morning and afternoon she could be found pushing her flower cart around the square, or sitting in the sun, awaiting a customer.

Her parents continued to sell the fruits and vegetables as they always did, on the same square. They were often visible to each other, while they remained worlds apart. The townspeople were aware of this breach, and often guessed correctly as to its cause. Still, it was not mentioned, except in the hushed tones of those who love to gossip.

Jacqueline had never considered leaving her home in Douai. It was all that she knew, and she was, after all, a woman alone. She also had the burden of the bells to deal with. She was never sure if her mission to bring back the bells was because it reminded her of happier times, or of falling in love.

Sometimes, her heart ached inside of her for the many things that she had lost in her life, and perhaps the bells were the only things that could *possibly* be restored. Maybe that would be enough.

The truth was that Jacqueline wanted to bring the bells back to Douai because the bells called her to do so. That point, and that point alone, was enough to guide her.

And so, she could often be seen moving about the square with her flower cart, helping the townspeople to believe that the bells would one day be restored.

It had been nearly eighteen years since the bells were taken from Douai. Jacqueline continued steadfastly in her mission.

In Dunkerque, the world is changing for Marc...

The dream was clearer than any other dream that Marc had ever known. Had he not awakened to find himself in his father's bed, in his own room, he would have thought it was real. The details remained clear as he swung his feet around the side of the bed to the floor.

As he looked out the solitary window that provided a view to the dock, he found that he was not seeing the docks at all, but he saw someone, presumably his father as a young man, in the town square of a distant village. He saw the steps of the town hall and he saw the vertical expanse of the building that he knew housed bells. He saw a gathering of people who all seemed to be engaged with each other, either disputing or agreeing on a single topic.

Marc wondered if, in his dream, he was seeing the village of his father's youth; or was it that, by lying in his father's bed, he had somehow taken on his father's dreams? Could it have been his father's spirit occupying his dreams? The thought of this both thrilled and scared Marc.

Whichever it was, Marc had an increasing and abiding sense that what he had experienced in the dream was not simply the random, reckless and disconnected musings of a mind at rest, but a journey or a direction.

When he finally stood, he took to straightening out the bed. He ran his hand over the smooth pouch, which covered the coarse material that made up the heap his father had used for a pillow for as long as Marc could remember. Marc wondered how his father could have found comfort in such a lumpy and misshapen mistake for a pillow.

He ran his hand slowly back and forth across the cover, as if he were trying to get to know this place where his father had laid his head. Marc felt a hard lump, and pushed against it. *Did his father keep rocks in his pillow?* he wondered.

Slowly, he slid his hand inside the pillow, reaching around until he found it: A small bit of metal, no bigger than his thumb. It appeared to be old. As Marc took all of it in, he turned it over slowly, getting to know it with his mind and his eyes, as well as with his fingers. It had the look and feel of the sort of rock that you sometimes see in the bed of a stream. It appeared as though there were edges that had once been sharp and jagged, but had since been worn smooth. Marc also recognized that it was not in the pillow by mistake. It was, without question, a keepsake of his father's possession: a small metal oval with a raised cross.

Marc's curiosity caused him to look about the room, inside and over and under things, exploring for other mementos that his father may have had. There were none.

Marc slid the metal object into his pocket. He had no idea of its worth, but he was somehow aware of its power. He was aware of it indeed, as he turned it over and over in his pocket as he walked aimlessly down the street.

Stopping for a reason that he did not understand, he withdrew the metal object and watched the sun land on it. He closed his fingers about it and felt the warmth of it. He kept it tightly there as he turned and walked toward the café. It was in his hand when he asked for tea, a slice of coarse bread and butter. It rested on the table in front of him as he slowly sipped the hot tea.

As he did so, he considered the idea that perhaps he would not return to work in the carpentry shop today, nor would he tomorrow, or any other tomorrows.

Marc sensed that his life had changed irrevocably. Alone, he began to feel the length of the days that were ahead of him. He was not fearful of them. He felt uneasy, as he understood that what he had always done, he would never do again, and that what he was about to embark on was as yet unknown to him. This sense of adventure was completely new to Marc. He had spent every day that he could remember in the close company of his father.

Now he was beginning to feel the way that he had felt in the dream, as though he was striding purposefully in an undefined direction, toward an unknown adventure. He was beginning to visualize it, when a stranger sat down at the café table along side of him.

"Tea and brown bread. A hearty start to the day! I believe that I will enjoy the very same."

The stranger said these things to Marc before he was even fully acquainted with the chair. Marc was startled more than surprised, so he responded with only a half smile. It was the next words from the man that brought the surprise: "Off on a journey, are you?"

The next few moments may have been just that, a few moments. But, they also could have been minutes or hours. Marc did not know.

In the small village where Marc had lived for the last fifteen years of his life, he knew who the villagers and the travelers were. He knew the look of a fisherman and the look of a wayfarer. He searched deeply into the man's face, trying to discern just which sort he was. He was not a villager, but also not a traveler, it seemed. His craggy features and balding head seemed somehow familiar or reminiscent to him, but he could not make a connection. Marc continued to search his face as he searched his thoughts about the question the man posed about his journey.

Every other day of his memory had been spent near the docks, in a carpentry shop, in the village that he had never left. He knew nothing of far-off lands, other than to overhear the bawdy stories that the fishermen sometimes told of places with exotic-sounding names.

His father had filled his head with no knowledge of the world, and had spoken vaguely and briefly of what he referred to only as "my home."

Even the few times when the extra glass of wine would loosen his tongue enough to mention the bells, or his young love, the details were sparing. Marc wished that he had wondered more and asked more about it, but he had not. He considered this fact: he had no real attraction for this village, other than to be in the company of his father, which he would never have again.

The sun, casting itself over the head of the stranger and directly into his eyes, forced Marc to redirect his gaze away from its glare and in the only direction he had ever looked: toward the ocean. For the first time, he found himself looking at the rolling hills that signaled the edge of the village and the larger hills beyond, which Marc considered the world's edge. He found himself thinking beyond the hills and wondering if on the other side was another village just like this one. Now, he felt the sense of wanting to know… a sense of wanderlust.

Looking back at the face of the stranger impassively, he could now easily recall where he had seen the man before. He had been there in his dream, popping up in this place and that, always looking at Marc with an expression that seemed to be just about to ask a question.

"A journey, yes…" was all that Marc said, and this made the man roar with laughter of approval.
"I knew it!" he said. "You have the look of a man off to make his mark upon the world."

Marc never once considered much of the world, let alone making a mark in it, but he responded with a weak "Yes" just the same.

"Yes, indeed. A journey…" the man said with his mouth halfway into his teacup.

As this was all occurring to Marc for the first time, he was not surprised that he would ask this question of the man:

"But where will I go, just over the hills?" he asked.

The stranger drained the cup and stood. It was just now that Marc observed his great height and recalled how his head was above all the others in the dream.

"You've got it wrong, son. When you know where you are going and when you will be returning, you are going on a trip. Do you know where you're going? Do you plan to return?"

As he said this, he picked up the metallic keepsake from the table and turned it over in his fingers. He bounced it a few times against his palm as if he were weighing it. As he replaced it on the table, he said the word "*bronze*" in a knowing fashion.

The empty tension as the questions hung unanswered in the air made it clear to Marc that he did not have to tell the man that the answer was no. There was no plan; he would not return.

"Then it's a journey, son. A journey is something that you follow. The thrill of the journey is *not* knowing where it will lead you. It is about leaving everything behind for something new. Do you have much to leave behind?" Knowing what the answer was, apparently by the look on Marc's face, encouraged the man to continue:

"Then I suspect that the journey has already begun."

Marc knew the answer to that question, and answered it with a boldness that surprised him: "It has."

The stranger, still standing, offered Godspeed to Marc and turned to walk away with a smile that seemed to conceal the knowledge of the world.

Marc turned toward the mountains and saw them now as a beginning rather than an ending.
He thought that he would tell this to the stranger, but when Marc turned back, the man was gone.

Thinking that he should get a few things, Marc returned to the room. He was surprised how barren it appeared to him. He went to the small leather pouch where his father stashed away the extra money, and tied it about his belt.

He then surveyed the room and decided to put his other shirt on top of the one he was wearing. He studied the contents of the room until his eyes landed on the only thing that had ever seemed to matter to his father: the bench where they played the bells.

Carrying the bench, Marc left for the carpentry shop. As he approached, he could see Claude sitting by the door. The wagon and mule that Claude used to bring the wood and deliver the furniture sat nearby, at the ready, although it had been years since Claude had made a trip alone.

"Your father rests with the undertaker. He waits for you to take him to the cemetery."

"Will you go with us, Claude?"

"I am too old for this trip, Marc."

"It is not so far, even for you."

Claude only smiled.

"What will I do now, Claude? Am I to stay here and continue working with you for all of my days?"

Claude allowed the question to fill the space between them, as he knew that this question was for Marc alone.

"If life is calling you away from this village, follow it with my blessing. Nevertheless, for today, you must deal with your father. Nothing more."

"I do not want to bury him, Claude."

"Why?"

"He will be alone. I have been to the cemetery, Claude. I have seen the markers. When people go there, they join their families. My father will be alone."

A long silence was finally ended when the old man said, "Take him home."

"But Claude, I know nothing of his home. I have never been there. Furthermore, how would I get him there?"

The old man motioned toward the mule and the cart that waited at the ready. Marc's stomach knotted. "He spoke of his home only a few times. He called it Douai."

"I know nothing of the world outside of Dunkerque, Claude. I would have no idea where this town is."

Claude stood slowly. Marc noticed that the years seemed to drain away from his face, as he stood erect and confident. Pointing in a certain direction over the hills, he said, "A two-day journey, maybe less. Take him home, son. Let him rest where he belongs."

Marc went with the cart to the undertaker's, where two boys lifted the casket and lashed it onto the cart. When Marc began to explain to the undertaker that his father would not be going to the cemetery in town, the man cut him off with these words:

"Claude told me last night that we need not dig a grave for your father."

Marc was puzzled by that comment, but said nothing to the undertaker. He checked to be sure that his load of a coffin and bench was secure, and set off in the direction which Claude had pointed.

As Marc considered the wisdom of the old man, he did so without thinking that he may never see him again. A journey of some two days might be either a wink or an eternity to someone who had never gone more than an hour from his home. Marc had no idea or any presuppositions of the journey. He just set off on it.

Marc arrives in Douai to bury his father...

He was surprised when he found himself in Douai. Given his cargo, he thought it best that he keep going without a stop. He was surprised that darkness had just fallen when he came to Douai.

The signpost that told him where he was also pointed in the direction of a church named for St. Theresa. It was there that he found the priest, Father Alphonse.

"I have brought my father to his home to be buried," he said quickly, after introducing himself. "What must I do now?"

"Does your family have a plot here at the church?"

"I know very little of my father's life as a boy. I know that he spoke of the bells and of Douai as his home. My father was a plain man, a carpenter."

"His family name?" the priest inquired.

"DuBois," Marc said, not knowing that this was the name that his father had created to hide his identity after he had taken him from the orphanage.

"There is no family of the church with such a name, son. I think that you are mistaken. Still, the holy church cares for its members. Who was your pastor in your own village?"

As the priest suspected, Marc had no answer for this.

"We have a pauper's field, son. Perhaps your father was from a farm nearby. If so, that would be his resting place."

In the morning, Marc dug the grave himself. It was a long and tear-filled job. Upon completion, he placed the bench alongside the newly turned earth.

When he was through, he "played" a song for his father; one that he knew his father loved, called "Papa's Lament". When he was done, he simply left the bench there and began to take the road back to Dunkerque.

Marc did not know, nor would he have guessed, that the bench was stolen before nightfall and was sold to a shop in Douai.

In the window, it caught the eye of Jacqueline, who took it home and placed it outside her flower shop. When she rested on it daily, she was never able to say exactly why it seemed oddly reminiscent to her.

As Marc left the town, Jacqueline could not have known that her own son, gone from her for nearly eighteen years, was leaving her own village after a very brief stay.

Marc's journey begins…

Marc was heading back to Dunkerque, or so he thought, until he began to feel uncertain about his reasons for returning. He realized it was all he knew, but began to believe that it was not enough. At the first place where the road split, he decided to go in the direction that would take him away from Dunkerque, and toward the unknown.

To his surprise, it was not long until he found himself in a village, not unlike the one where he had lived. This one, however, was not alongside the sea and did not have the aroma of the sea that had filled his nostrils every day. Instead, he enjoyed the smell of heather until it was replaced by the smell of dark coffee. He followed the fragrance to the patisserie and sat quietly in a chair by the window with a cup of coffee and some dark bread that was unlike what he knew. *Sweeter,* he thought. For the first time, he carefully counted out the money that he had and was pleased with the amount.

A gruff voice surprised him with the words, "A rich man, I see!" He smiled and quietly shook his head at the baker, a burly man with large arms and a thick torso. Proudly, Marc left the small leather pouch on the table.

"Perhaps you should be enjoying our finest sweets, rich man."

It surprised Marc that the man spoke to him with such familiarity, and so he felt more comfortable than he often did around strangers.

"It is not so very much, and it must last me a long time. I am on a journey."

"Yes, a traveler. I should have known. Can you not stay some time in our village?"

Marc did not know if he would be staying or not. He was new to being a traveler. The baker directed a question to a man who was sitting, quite inconspicuously, in the corner:

"Do you think that he would enjoy our village?"

The man seemed thoughtful when he said, "Those on a journey always need to get to the next village."

"I suppose so," the baker said, speaking about Marc, but not to him.

"I once wished that I could travel, but now I cannot. Who will feed the village, if not me?" This he said only to Marc.

"Well, traveler, let me make a gift to you. Come into the back and I will wrap some bread and a sweet for your journey. Then you will remember our village well."

At first, Marc was unsure if the baker was speaking to him or to the other man. But, when the baker said, "Come," as he waved toward him, Marc was only too anxious to enjoy the generosity of the baker. He was thinking that a journey might be a good thing.

Once in the back, the baker seemed to want to show Marc the oven and the huge bowls, and the wooden casks that held the milk and the cream. From time to time, he would look over Marc's shoulder. Marc supposed the baker was checking for new customers.

He was very deliberate in taking thick brown paper and very carefully wrapped a small loaf of bread and a sweet croissant into it, and then tied a tight knot around the package.

"For your journey, traveler." he said, and Marc thanked him enthusiastically.

"How much?" he asked, wanting to be sure that he had not mistaken the hospitality.

"Ahhh… it is my gift to you."

Returning to the front of the patisserie, Marc noticed immediately that the man was gone. It was a moment before he noticed that his money was also gone. "My money! It is all that I have!" Marc was shouting as he ran outside and looked up and down the street for the missing man. He knew instantly that he would not see him again.

He ran back into the patisserie, arms flailing. "What will I do?" he implored of the baker. The baker wore an odd expression of guilt. It was a look that Marc recalled from the many times he would go to the mill to pick up the boards, and the count was always wrong. In his instant recognition and anger, Marc screamed, "You were in on it, too!"

"You accuse me!" the baker roared, as he took a step toward Marc. "You gypsy!"

Marc was gone in an instant. He walked faster and faster, until he found himself running. He did so until he could feel some distance between himself and the village.

When he stopped, he was aware that he had instinctively run toward home and that the mule and wagon had been left behind. He was more sad than angry. Standing with his hands on his hips and his chest heaving, he tried to regain his breath. He looked toward his home, then back toward the hills.

His first instinct was to head home to the comfort of what he knew. When he turned to go in the other direction, it was because he was afraid not to.

When he came back near the village of his misfortune, he skirted around the edge of it, and felt relieved when it was at his back again. The wagon track that he followed wound endlessly toward the top of the next hill. Marc hoped that there would be less adventure over it.

Marc contemplated the fact that he had left the mule and the wagon behind. Although it seemed like a reckless act, he was glad that he had shed himself entirely of his former life. He also knew that every time that he looked back toward the cart, it would have reminded him of its sad cargo.

When he came to the top of the hill, it was night. He could see nothing, not even the path in front of him. And so, with the full realization that he was a man without a home, he took a few steps toward the cover of a tree, and laid his head amidst a mossy spot. At first, he began to sleep the intense sleep of the weary traveler. Then, he began to dream… to dream where all men are kings.

In the dream, Marc walked endlessly. He was happy as he saw himself whistling and going from village to village. He would stop at the cafés, greet the people and get to know them and their ways. He would stroll through the markets and survey the fruits. At each village, someone would offer him their most delicious fruit with the words, "For you, traveler." He would thank them and smile. Then, they would ask, "Where are you going, traveler?" He would always answer them by simply saying, "Home." Then, he would head toward another village. When he arrived, he would always enjoy the views and the folks, but he carried the abiding sense that he would not be staying. He was always heading toward a home that he feared existed only in his imagination.

When he awoke, it was as though the dream continued. Marc was less settled and more fearful than in his dreaming. Still he walked, following only the sense that the next place might welcome him home. When the road would offer two choices, there was never a dilemma. He would always seem to know which choice was right for him, without a thought.

He walked until the sun became distant beyond the horizon. Several times, he stopped to eat a piece of fruit. As he did so, he considered his direction more than his destination. He tried to tell himself that he was not lost, but searching. He set himself down beneath a roadside tree. He was tired, and hoped that he would find a village by nightfall. It did not seem as though he would.

He sat quietly, wondering if he should walk a bit further in the hope of seeing the lights of a town, or just stay there. He heard several shouts, seemingly of happiness. Or was it alarm?
He walked in the direction of the sounds, but he heard nothing further to guide him until he saw someone standing by the bend of an inviting stream.

He called to the person but got no response, so he walked closer. He walked directly up to a man who was holding a fish in his hands, and staring.

"Hello," was all that Marc could think to offer.

The man answered without looking up at first.

"I have caught this beautiful fish. I was hungry, but now when I look at it, I cannot decide if I should eat it or not. It is a gorgeous fish, is it not?"

As he said this, he looked up into Marc's face. As he did, the fish flapped around in the man's grasp, enough to startle him and cause him to laugh loudly from his belly. The man wiped his hand down the side of his trousers and extended it to Marc with warmth and a smile.

"My name is Didier. You seem a stranger to Tourcoing."

"I am on a journey, I suppose. My name is Marc." His voice trailed off… as he did not know what else to say, but had no wish to leave. There seemed to be something about this man, Didier, which Marc enjoyed.

"I can build a fire for you, if you like," Marc said. The man considered this, but when the fish flapped again with a little less enthusiasm, he bent over and released the fish into the water. They both watched it, as it seemed to lie there for a few moments. Then, with a strong flap of its tail, it was gone.

"He's going home, I suppose," the man said.

"I suppose so…" Marc said, his voice trailing off again. Marc surprised himself when he asked of the man, "Where is your home?"

The man pointed beyond a stand of trees to a small cabin. "Yours?" he asked Marc.

"Since I was a young boy, I lived with my father in Dunkerque. When he died, I left my village."

"So, where are you going?"

"I do not know, sir. I am lost, and yet, I am not lost. I am happy, and I am distracted. The only thing that I know for sure is that I continue to walk away from my home and toward something…"

"Why not just go home?"

Marc knew it was a fair question that any reasonable person would ask. It was the *answer* that he continually avoided thinking about. After a few thoughtful moments, he began to respond, unaware that as he did so, the answer would come to him.

"I lived there with my father. It was just he and I. When he died, I felt that I no longer belonged there."

"What about your family? If it was your father's home, then there must be others, no?"

The question somehow pierced through many years. "It was not my father's home. It was where we settled."

"In all of those years, you and your father never began to call it home?"

"My father never acted as though he was home. He established few relationships, built no proper home, and acquired nothing material to speak of. We lived in a single room at the top of a hotel."

Didier asked the obvious question: "Why?"

"I know very little because my father said very little. I know that he fled his home after it became occupied. I know that he loved the bells of that town so much that he was heartbroken when they were destroyed. While he relaxed, he would occasionally speak of the time before we came to Dunkerque, but it was not really about a town or village or farm. He would speak of the bells and their music, and his eyes would close as he did so. You could see his entire countenance change as he went there in his memory.

To my father, the bells *were* home. That is what he left for me, a love for the music of the bells...bells that are no longer there until you squeeze your eyes so tightly that you can hear them, you can feel them, and you can play them.

The bells were my father's home, and they are my heritage, I suppose. He left me no property and no direction. All that he left me was an empty room and a dream of bells."

Marc was surprised when Didier replied, "He has left you a great deal."

"Really?" Marc said, scoffing.

"Son, you say that he has left you without a home, but your heart is filled with music and dreams. His home was with the bells...bells that were taken from him. Can you not see that the burning in your chest to find your home is the thing that he left to you? Can you not see that he spent many years *not* making your home in a small room? Can you not see that he left you wanting for more, and *that* is something that you must find for yourself?"

Didier's voice was thundering now. He was speaking to Marc in the way that a disapproving father speaks to his son:

"Tell me the rest of it. No father would leave his son without at least one memento to remind him of the past and guide him into the future. What did he leave to you?"

"A bench and bit of metal!" Marc screamed. "Nothing of any earthly use or value."

"Tell me about the bench."

Marc described the bench to Didier and told him how his father would sit on it and imagine the bells.

"And this bench, was this where your father was when he was happiest?"

"Yes."

"Where is it now?"

"I left it by his grave. It was all that he had."

"You didn't need it?"

"No."

"But this bench... it became a kind of home to you both?"

"Yes! When I sat on it and played the bells, I would feel as though I was leaving our little room and the village that always smelled of fish and sawdust. I know that my father did, too."

"And the bit of metal?"

Marc did not know what it was, except that it was a shiny bit of metal that his father had worn smooth from rubbing. He could do nothing but remove it from its safe place and hand it to Didier.

"Bronze!" the man said instantly. "Bronze: the only fitting metal for a bell."

"He said that the bells of his home were destroyed. Perhaps this is a bit of them?" Marc asked.

Didier only smiled.

"Your father *has* left you a great deal."

Marc was thinking too hard about what Didier meant to come to any sort of understanding. He looked at him, unable to hide the fact that he was perplexed.

"Your father left you hope. Hope can be a map, if we are willing to divine its direction...if we are called to the unknown. Is something calling to you, son?"

Marc nodded anxiously, hoping that a man so wise would give him the answer.

Didier asked again, "What did your father leave you?"

"An empty bench and a piece of a bell that was destroyed long ago."

"Perhaps the bells have been replaced," Didier said.

"Perhaps the bench is empty," Marc said, in a voice that came to him without thought or effort.

Marc and Didier walked away from the edge of the stream together. They walked until they came to the edge of the road that Marc had been traveling on.

"I need to return, and I know that you need to go on," said Didier. He slapped Marc on the shoulder in a way that directed him up the hill from where they were standing.

"Thank you," Marc said, after his second step. Didier smiled, but this was hidden to Marc now, as Didier was walking away in the other direction. He only saw him raise his hand to wave goodbye.

Marc did not look back again. He was hoping to cross the little mountain that was the only barrier in front of him. *Perhaps, there will be a village in the next valley,* he thought to himself.

Marc's journey continues...

Marc spent a lot of time thinking of his father, and bells, and mysteries, and his own undirected life. His thoughts came to rest on the belief that he must find bells. He lived nomadically, yet happily for the next eight years.

He would travel about, take some work for a month or so and then move on. Always, he would inquire about towns with bells.

After Marc began to hear the name of one particular place several times, and the name of a certain carillonneur from that same town even more, he made it his destination.

Many twists and turns of little villages and towns brought him, finally, to a place called St. Amand-les-Eaux. It was an intimidating place to young Marc, particularly when he saw the huge towers of the abbey that seemed to rule over the town. The tallest, more than twenty-five meters higher than the others, was the home of the bells. It was also the home of the carillonneur of St. Amand and his family. The carillonneur's name was Jacques Lannoy.

Timidly, Marc sought out the carillonneur, and was relieved to find him to be a man who humbled himself in the shadow of the great bells.
Marc was direct in his question:

"Can you teach me to play the bells?"

"I do not know. Why do you ask this of me?"

Deciding to keep much of his life's story to himself, Marc said only this: "I have had their music in my head for as long as I can remember. Sometimes, it seems that the world is conspiring to bring the bells and me together, as if they are to be my guide."

Jacques was intrigued by his answer, and responded: "I offer what I can. Sometimes I am learning to play the bells, and sometimes I teach them. Sometimes the student seems interested, but the bells refuse. On some days, it seems that the bells are my master, and on others days, they are a willing servant. Stay here if you like. We will see if the bells are looking for a student."

Marc's life in St. Amand begins…

Marc was able to find work readily as a woodworker, which enabled him to procure a modest room of his own, at the very top of the Hotel Au Chateau Des Thermes.

It was modest indeed, as it generally served as a large closet. But, Marc was happy to have a place in the city, up high, near where the bells lived.

As instructed, he waited for Jacques to summon him, but he heard nothing from the carillonneur. After a long three months, he finally mustered his courage and sought out the teacher.

"Will I have a chance to study with you?"

"Yes, I suppose."

"I have heard nothing from you. How long must I wait?"

"How long are you prepared to wait?"

"As long as I must, teacher."

"Well then, if waiting is what you are prepared to do, then I shall let you wait."

Marc returned from the abbey in great disappointment. But, he remained determined to study with Jacques Lannoy.

He would walk the town, getting to know his new surroundings. As he did, he would take in the sounds of the carillon when it played.

He was surprised to learn that although the note of each bell remained unchanged from day to day, and sometimes the same melodies would play, they sounded different from one day to the next. Sometimes, he noted that his mind would drift away from the music altogether.

Other days, the song captured his mind, his heart and his imagination completely. Sometimes, he would notice a wrong note being struck. He would smile as he began to understand that on some days, the bells were being played by Jacques, and on other days by one of his students.

Marc would arrogantly convince himself that he would make a better student than some he heard, as he was impatient for his chance.

He discovered that Jacques, the Master, always played on Sundays. Marc would lie on the cot that he had shoved next to the window and take in each impassioned note from the tower. He began to notice how the bells could take control of his own emotions. He knew that how the final piece was played, be it dreamy, sorrowful, joyous or militant, would define his own feelings throughout the day.

Sometimes, he would sit on the edge of his cot and strike the notes that he was hearing, just as he had done with his father long ago. On some of these occasions, he could feel the actual presence of his father with him, standing just over his right shoulder.

When the presence was strongest, Marc always resisted turning to look because he wanted to avoid the reality that his father was not there.

Months passed…then seasons. Marc had not heard a thing from Jacques. He busied himself with his carpentry work. Although the bells never left his mind entirely, he had begun to notice that he thought about them a little less each day. He found this to be disquieting, but was unsure what he could do about it.

On a particular Sunday, Marc positioned himself to listen. The bells were lilting at the start, and then seemed to gain momentum and spirit. He closed his eyes during a dreamy piece as his head moved slowly from side to side.

His feet swung around the side of the bed as the music changed and sang to him of love. It brought him to his feet and he began to dance, first as if he were a child, and then as if he were a man holding his lover.

The music paused, only for a moment.
The piece, unknown to Marc, was beautiful in its somber melody. It froze him where he stood. His imagination carried him outside the window, beyond the town, past the forest, and all the way back to his most distant memory: being carried by his father for a seemingly endless amount of time. He remembered the wordless journey and how he felt secure and safe for the very first time.

The music continued, melancholic now. He recalled the sad journey of taking his father to Douai, where he buried him in a paupers' field.

As Marc began to cry, he realized it had been years since he cried for his father. He fought the tears at first, but then they came so completely, pulled from him by the song, that he could only yield to them. He sobbed, like a man gasping for air while drowning.

Finally, when it felt as though he could cry no more, the music paused. In the momentary silence, he felt as though he had been emptied of something vile.

As the music changed again, it began to fill his heart with a sense of something that he could only identify as triumph, and he noticed that he was moving and then quickening his pace, almost at a run, around his tiny room.

After circling the room twice, he burst through the door. During his flight down the stairway, his feet barely touched the wooden steps. He ran through the town, continuously being lifted up and sped along by the song of triumph that was pouring into each of his senses. He followed the notes, as if they were the sweet smells from a patisserie that filled your nostrils and drew you to them.

His running was urgent and he made no pause at the foot of the bell tower. He bounded up all three hundred and forty-seven steps until he stood there, just a meter away from Jacques. Jacques seemed to be inside of his music and made no motion or action to acknowledge that he was aware of Marc's presence.

When the piece ended, his hands rested on his knees and his head dipped down nearly to the keys. When he turned to look at Marc, there was no look of surprise, only a look of welcome.

It was Marc that was surprised. The silence of the bells caused him to wonder how and why he had so urgently come to this spot. He stared wordlessly at Jacques, who looked back at him without revealing any thought or emotion.

When Marc first tried to speak, he could only stutter, and so he stopped.

The words that finally came from him seemed to be a relief to Jacques, but were a surprise to Marc, as they fell of their own accord from his lips.

"I cannot wait any longer, teacher. I cannot."

Jacques smiled, and then said, "Finally. It is finally time for you to begin."

And so it began…

Jacques teaches Marc...

"Tell me," Jacques asked, "Why do you want to play the bells?"

"My father studied the bells at his home. He apprenticed there for several years. When he left his home, he and I lived in Dunkerque and worked together as carpenters. He spoke very little of his boyhood, his home or my mother. Actually, he spoke very little of the bells, also. But, it was the bells that he longed for."

"How do you know about this longing?"

"I saw him change as he played the bells."

"You confuse me, Marc. There is no carillon in Dunkerque."

"True. He fashioned his own way to play it and that is how he taught me."

Jacques only stared at Marc, not knowing what to say or ask. Marc was beginning to feel a bit foolish and unsure of how to explain himself. He was, however, beginning to understand that playing bells on wooden pegs as you sing the notes was going to sound ridiculous to Jacques. And so he just shook his head, and began to stare at his feet.

"How did he teach you?"

It took courage for Marc to respond in the way that he did. He improved his posture on the chair where he sat, positioned his feet, and then closed his hands into the fists of a carillonneur ready to play.

"My father put pegs into the wall, just like those," he said, pointing to the carillon keyboard that was immediately behind Jacques. "He marked the floor where the pedals would be and then he taught me the position of each note. He would play in this way and I would listen. As I grew older, I would learn the melodies and would watch his every move. One day, as he slept on his cot, I began to mimic him, although my feet barely reached the floor. I played what I had heard, singing the notes as he had done. I was unaware that I had awakened him, until I felt him standing behind me, coaxing and encouraging me."

Marc then played the imaginary keys, singing them as he did so: "Bum-bum-bum-bum-bum."

Then he stopped, noticing the incredulous look, followed by a broad smile on Jacques' face. "That is how he taught you?"

"Yes, and that is how he played the bells as well."

Marc smiled at the memory, as he explained how his father would tap him on the head or shoulder when he would strike a note incorrectly. He explained how his father would sing the note that he had played to demonstrate that it was incorrect and then show him the correct key.

"And where is your father now?"

"When he died, I decided to take him to the home that he sometimes mentioned, a journey of a few days from Dunkerque, to a place called Douai. He seemed to be unknown there, and his name was unfamiliar to the priest. Even when I asked about the bells, I learned nothing, as the priest told me that there were no bells in Douai."

"What was his name?"

"DuBois…" And then, after a pause, he said, "Henri DuBois."

Clearly, Jacques was confused and curious at the story. His eyes revealed only questions as he looked at Marc. His response was this:

"I must know something, Marc. Come with me."

Learning the carillon is difficult. It is simply not possible for some people to convert tons of bronze bells into delicate song. Most students give up long before they approach any sense of mastery, even after years of trying. To keep students from punishing the townspeople with their inadequacy, most bell towers include a practice keyboard where students play a simulated carillon. Rather than strike bells, the clappers strike metal plates of the correct notes. The mistakes do not punish the listeners' ears as the students learn and progress.

Every student that Jacques ever mentored, and every student that he had ever known learned first on the piano. Then, after mastering that instrument, the student would begin work with the practice carillon. It was clear to Jacques that this particular student had never touched a piano, because he made no mention of it.

Every instinct was telling him that Marc had a clear love and passion for the bells, but no knowledge of music at all. He knew that it would be sensible to begin teaching him the piano to see if he possessed talent along with his desire. But instead, he sat Marc at the practice carillon without further instruction.

Marc ran his fingers over the wooden keys as if he were trying to get to know them on a deeper level. He felt at home here, on this bench at the top of this tower. He had no thought in his head of impressing the teacher. He simply yearned to play. At first, he struck the five notes that he always did. As he did so, he sang the notes that he heard coming from the tuned metal bars.

To the surprise of Jacques, they matched. To Marc, it was what he expected. With deliberate strokes, Marc played. After a measure or so, he stopped singing the notes, as it was now unnecessary.

When the song ended, Marc was obviously enthralled and Jacques was speechless. Excitedly, and without turning to face him, Marc said:

"I loved that last piece you played this morning. It made me run and smile."

Then, he played it, perhaps not with the mastery and fluidity of Jacques, but far better than any other student ever had.

When the piece ended and Jacques began to comprehend what was occurring, Marc swung his legs around to face Jacques.

"Do you know that piece?" Jacques asked in disbelief.

"Oh, no. I just played what I remembered from this morning when you played it so beautifully."

The task of a teacher is to find a way to transfer knowledge to a student. Jacques knew this better than most. He also knew that he must inspire his students.

But, his experience had never caused him to encounter such a mysterious prodigy as Marc. Jacques was delighted to have this curious young man as a student, all the while knowing that Marc's gift for the carillon, as unexplainable as it was, exceeded his own.

He also had never seen anyone who delighted in endless hours on the practice instrument or who possessed the gift of flawlessly playing what he heard.

He wondered how much of this gift was passed to him from his father, how much was God-given, and how much was imparted to him from the spirit of the bells.

Jacques began to teach Marc how to play from sheets of music, which presented a fair level of difficulty to the student. Over time, Marc learned to translate the notes on the page to the notes of the bells accurately, but without the passion that he felt when he played only from his heart.

To teach, a teacher should maintain a certain level of separation of duties between himself and his pupil. But, in ways that Jacques had never experienced before, Marc became like a son. It was a relationship that they both engaged in without thought or words.

Marc's life in St. Amand continues...

For the first two years of his tutelage, Marc was a visitor to the tower almost daily. Then, Jacques noticed that Marc had lost a little bit of the gloomy air that sometimes hung over him. At the same time, his rehearsals became less frequent.

When Jacques mentioned this to his wife, Françoise, she made it instantly apparent to Jacques what was causing Marc to be less immersed in the carillon, yet happier. Following their time together one afternoon, Jacques asked him bluntly:

"Am I correct in sensing that there is love in your life?'

Surprised by the question, the normally shy Marc began to rattle on endlessly about Estelle and how they spent their time together.

Estelle was a girl of the city, far more sophisticated than Marc, and a lover of music. Estelle was tall and had an elegant manner. She had been properly schooled by parents who had been asking, quite often, about her prospects for marriage.
She knew of literature and of foreign places, and had been educated to speak in other languages. Estelle knew the history of her country, and could name every fountain in France. Marc found her exotic and fascinating.

When Jacques inquired as to Estelle's family, Marc would only say that they were fine people who were people of means. Beyond that, Marc really did not know, and had no particular interest in that topic.

Marc was at a disadvantage of which he was unaware. Estelle was quite aware of it, but did not understand it. Loving parents, along with the help of a considerable staff, had raised Estelle. Her many hours of reading had inspired her with the hopes of romance.

Marc had neither the background in literature nor the family background that would have provided him with any kind of model for companionship, romance, or for love itself. It is true that he was enamored by Estelle, but had never made any kind of physical advances.

Estelle longed for more than the conversations and the long walks. She often experienced the playful ways that her father demonstrated affection for her mother. Marc had seen none of this, having been raised solely by his father. He sought only to win Estelle's approval.

"I have promised Estelle that when I begin to play the actual carillon, I will play for her. Am I far from that day, Jacques?"

Jacques had wondered when this request would come to him. His other students were far less capable than Marc, but were constantly asking to play the tower bells. Marc seemed so content to play the practice carillon that Jacques thought it best to wait until his student wanted to perform for the city. Still, the wise teacher recognized that Marc wanted to play only to impress, which he knew was not enough.

"Your time is coming, Marc. I think that the three of us will know when that day arrives."

"The three of us?"

"Me, you, and, of course, the bells."

Marc, in his complete trust of the teacher, seemed to accept the answer. As the next two years passed, it became apparent to Jacques that he had nothing left of the bells to teach Marc. Still, he knew that Marc had more to learn.

It was in life itself that the teacher took to raising Marc. He made no encouragement for Marc to play the actual carillon; he would wait until Marc yearned for it.

In long and slow conversations, he would tell him that the bells have a life that is inspired by the carillonneur. His mission was to align himself in spirit with the bells, the heavens, the music and ultimately, and of paramount importance, to those who would listen. Marc would try to understand.

"When you play a song of love, Marc," he would say, "It must *become* a song of love… to those who listen. Otherwise, it is no more than a pretty collection of notes."

Marc would nod dutifully.

"When the song is a song of loss, you must be feeling a loss from your own life, and tell it to the bells. Then, and only then, will you be telling it to those on the ground. A song of victory must be played by a victor; a song of praise must be played by a believer."

Marc understood. He recalled it in his father's face. He remembered it in the day that Jacques had played so beautifully that the music called him, in bounding steps, to the tower. But, he could not play it. He could not feel it. Both teacher and student knew it.

Still, they rehearsed and Marc improved. He even mentioned to his master that he hoped he would spend the rest of his days at St. Amand, one day replacing his teacher as the carillonneur. Jacques would always smile and only respond, "We shall see."

On a clear day in October, Marc and Estelle walked alone near the hot springs. Marc, being no man of the world, delighted in every moment that he and Estelle spent together and all that she taught him. When he spoke to her of the future, it was always a distant place where they would be married and together. But he had no plan, and Estelle could accurately see that Marc was perfectly content with his life just as it was. She made allowances for her shy and sensitive lover, knowing of a distant father and the fact that he never knew his mother. She knew that he had not been raised in the shadow of affection and love shared by husband and wife, as she herself had been.

She even nudged him carefully from time to time regarding improving his status through his work as a carpenter or with the bells that he loved so much. But, she was far too subtle for Marc to comprehend. The clock that ticks in the mind of a twenty-three year old woman was nonexistent to Marc.

With the kindest words that she could create, she told Marc that she was leaving her home.

"Where will you go?"

"To Nice."

"Nice?"

"Yes. It is a town on the southern side of our country, near Italy. It will take a journey of many days."

"Why?"

"My parents think it best."

"And you, Estelle, what do you think?"

"I must agree with them. It is time to move on in my life. I am no longer a young girl."

Without hesitation, Marc said, "Then I shall go, too."

"You cannot, Marc. I go to marry another."

Although Estelle had not planned to be so blunt, she was relieved when the words left her.

"My parents have made arrangements."

To say that the world was crashing in for Marc would be to say too little. His senses were stripped. His mind was blank and swirling at the same time. His feet wanted to move, but he remained in one spot.

"But I thought that *we* would marry!" Marc was angered and bewildered as he said these words.

Estelle loved Marc enough to understand what he did not know. She cared enough to want to comfort him, but did not know how.

She stood by him, quietly and patiently, until she decided to speak to him in the way that she felt: anxious from the endless waiting with which he was so comfortable. The words were instantly clear in his understanding as she said them:

"When, Marc? When? When the bells tell you?"

And she was gone from him.

After Estelle turned away from Marc, he began to walk. He walked until he was deep into the forest and sat down, exhausted. When the tears came, he welcomed them. When the bells began to play that evening, they rang a light-hearted melody, which angered him. There was no room in his heart for joy.

When he left the forest that evening, it was nearly dark. He had no wish to return to his room. The normal feeling of solitude that he enjoyed there made him fear that the loneliness would consume him.

It was a month before Marc extracted himself from the numbing effects of the constant consumption of wine.

Marc wanders aimlessly around St. Amand...

Marc had no idea what he had done wrong. At first, he felt as though Estelle had wronged him without cause. It drained all desire from him. He made no trips to the carpentry shop where he was expected. He gave no thought or care for the furniture that people waited for him to complete. Also, he disregarded the bells.

He was in this state when he came to a café, and quickly procured a wine of deep red. The likeness to blood appealed to him in a strangely macabre fashion. He sat alone and finished the glass of wine quickly. When the second glass was emptied, his tears began to come again. Unable to hold them back or remain silent, he was sobbing softly with his sleeve covering his mouth as a muffler, when a stranger joined him at the table.

The man asked for no invitation and he made no immediate effort at conversation. Marc felt unable to ask him to go away, and so they sat in silence long after the tears subsided.

"I, too, have had my heart broken..." the man said, letting the words linger.

When Marc began to speak, he surprised himself. He told the stranger of how Estelle had left him, when surely she knew that some day he would marry her.

He continued explaining how she must have known that he had not yet arrived in the place in his life where he could care for a wife and the children that would follow. He told him how they spoke effortlessly about everything, and that Estelle never had spoken of any urgency regarding their common plans. "She deceived me," he said.

The old man looked at Marc with pity.

"No, son, she did not. You put her feet to sleep."

The instant and surprising recognition that this was true brought no comfort to Marc. The anger that he instantly felt toward himself, he directed toward the old man. With a look of defiance, Marc reached across the table, enveloping the man's throat in his grasp. "You know nothing!" he yelled repeatedly, each time tightening his grasp on the man's neck.

With great effort, the others at the café rescued the man by prying Marc's hands from him. When a barrel-chested man wrapped Marc into a bear hug, Marc fought back consistently and vigorously until he was completely spent.

When the older man was safely away and Marc began to weaken, the man let him go. Marc collapsed into a pile at his feet. He then began to return the wine to the ground, with loud retching noises.

The café owner wasted no time in throwing the unyielding Marc to the street, with the words "*un ivrogne!*" as he waved his index finger past his nose.

That was the state that Marc remained in for thirty days. Drunk. Over and over, he experienced the loss of Estelle. Sometimes, he would cry for his father. When he would begin to feel something approaching sobriety, clearer thoughts would remind him that he did nothing to fuel the love or the hopes of the woman that he adored. He could not deny that he had simply paid too little attention to her feelings. When he became drunk again, he would call Estelle the vilest of things.

After a while, there was no café in St. Amand that did not block his entry.

Slipping about in the black night, he would find a flask or bottle to steal and take it with him to the forest. He would be tortured by the drink and his own memories, and finally, the truth.

Marc found himself awakening in the spot where he had collapsed in the forest the previous night.

At first, he thought that consuming too much wine and not enough food caused the burning in his body. Soon enough, he recognized the feel of a boot in his belly. When he grabbed the leg attached to the boot, it did not yield.

Trying to pull his attacker down became pointless and ultimately horrifying, as he looked up into the face of his own father. He saw no pity in his father's face, only the warm smile that he recognized when his father sat at the bench. He reached his arms up toward his father, as if he were begging, and asked him, "What am I to do?"

He was surprised when his father roared in laughter and then mimicked his words, using the voice of a child.

It stung Marc to hear this. As he stared up at him, he watched the face transform from that of his father into the dirty and grizzled face of the people that robbed others and used the forest as a refuge.
He saw the face of his father disappear just before a boot landed on his jaw. He would remain there, motionless, throughout all of that day until the next night.

It was the bells that woke him...

He sat up slowly, trying to identify all the places that were bringing him pain. The ground where his head had been was soaked in red, from both wine and blood. The wine was gone, and he had no ill feelings from the loss of it.

Making his way to the nearby stream, he immersed his head quickly and completely. As he removed his head from the water to dunk it again, his own image in the water was frightening.

As his ears became submerged, he could still hear the bells, tormenting him all the more. After dipping his head in the cool water repeatedly, he lingered there on his hands and knees, listening to the bells and feeling sickened by his own reflection.

When the song ended, Marc walked slowly back to his room. Along the way, he made the simple but necessary decision that he could not continue in this way.

At the hotel, he bathed and then he slept. Then, he headed to see Jacques. He hoped that Jacques would understand and comfort him. He longed for his wisdom.

Jacqueline at the square in Douai...

A woman spoke out, "Jacqueline, we know that you believe. But, it is only a few days until Christmas and there is no one to play for the festival. Why should we continue to believe, as you do?"

It would be fair to say that for many of the people of Douai, they wished that Jacqueline would simply let the past die away. Of course, she could not.

"I do not know why you should believe. But, I can tell you why *I* do. Don't you remember how it all began with Laurent, the sea captain? If you do not, then let me remind you of how we got our bells back. Let me remind you of why I believe:

It was some years ago that the foreigners left us, having destroyed our bells and having made war with our people. All that remained were bad memories, bitter fears, and six cannons in the field. As time passed, all remnants of the soldiers' camp disappeared, save those cannons.

Some of the men spoke about how the foreigners had made the giant fires and re-fashioned the bells into cannons. Although they knew that they had no knowledge of how to cast the metal back into bells, they made several futile efforts to smelt the cannons.

Seeing them in any other shape at all would have been preferable to seeing the soul of our city as weapons, with weeds growing around and inside of them.

It was futile. Large fires were built around the cannons, but they refused to budge. When we heard about this, many of us, including me, believed that there would never be bells again. As was often said, the bells had been up in that tower since Moses was a young boy.

So it was, until the sea captain came to Douai on a particular market day to buy wine and cheese for his next voyage. He had been coming to Douai for many, many years."

Jacqueline waited, wanting to be certain that they were all listening.

"Captain Laurent came to market. We all knew that he had been here before. He was such a happy and boisterous man of immense size. He fancied both our cheese and our wine. Whenever he put into port and had the time to do so, he would come by wagon to load up on them both for the next voyage. He often said that the cheese alone was worth the journey of two days. There were times when he would sit in the square, eating one hunk of cheese after another, sipping wine and telling sea stories to all who would listen. Sometimes, it seemed that he would devour every ounce that was intended for his next journey.

One night, as the dusk began to settle in, he said that he would gladly succumb to sleep, but he loved to hear the bells of our town as he drifted off.
The wine had apparently removed many years from his memory.

One of the men quickly exclaimed, 'The bells are gone, Monsieur. They took them a long time ago.'

'Who would steal bells?' the captain asked, his eyes searching all present.

I said, 'Soldiers came and took them… foreigners. But then, we drove them away.'

'A sad tale, sadder than all of mine,' the captain said thoughtfully.

The captain looked directly at me, and asked, 'Will you not bring back the bells?'

'We tried, Monsieur,' I answered, 'but our men simply do not know how. We have tried and we have failed.'

'Surely, someone can make bells,' said Captain Laurent. 'Were they not made before, by the hands of men?'

'Indeed,' I replied. 'But, the bells had been in the tower for hundreds of years.'

The captain rose slowly. He nudged his driver and they made ready to leave. I then asked, 'Will you not spend the night?'

'Suddenly, it seems that I cannot. I know a man, you see…' his voice trailed off in a mischievous way.

The last thing he said was, 'Your name again, Madame?'

I had barely said it, when he was off.

Several months later, a stranger was inquiring in the town about me. I knew this, but since I did not know the nature of his interest, I watched and waited.

In a few days, he came and addressed me by name, saying that he had business to discuss with me.

'What business?' I asked, knowing that my voice gave away my fear. Some people from the village had warned me that a foreign man was looking for me. Though it had been years since our occupation, there was never a day we lived without fear.

'Captain Laurent came to see me. He said that it was time for me to meet my destiny.'

'And so?' I asked.

'You need bells. I need to unload this heavy debt from my heart. Can we make a deal?'

'Monsieur, you puzzle me,' I said.

'Do you need bells, woman? Are you not Jacqueline?'

'Yes.'

Then he laughed, making me feel foolish.

A long silence followed. The man looked nervously about, thinking deeply, it seemed.

Then, he began: 'I am Paul. Since I was a boy, I worked in Dresden, a town far from here. I apprenticed there, and learned my trade as a foundry man. This had been my life, except for the time that I served in the army.

Although I had come to loathe my work as a foundry man, it did not bring me the shame and guilt that I felt when I was a soldier.

I left the army in shame and found work in a shipyard, but I did not return to my native Dresden. I felt as though I could not. Instead, I found work in the ports of France. I would work long and hot hours, casting the metal parts for the ships. I made the huge anchors and many of the parts that required casting from molten iron and bronze. Of course, we also made the ships' bells, which became the only part of my work that I enjoyed.

One day, many years ago, a captain came to me and asked that I repair the largest of his ship's bells that had been cracked. I suspected that this was caused by poor workmanship, plus the effects of its life in the changing climes of the sea.

I agreed, telling the captain that it would take some time. He agreed to call for it in six weeks when he returned to port.

The captain could not have known that I had spent nearly every day since I was a boy making parts for the ships on which I dreamed of sailing. I dreamed of distant and exotic places. But most of all, I dreamed of leaving the eternal and infernal heat of my craft. I thought my plan was a brilliant one.

Rather than repair the bell, I used it to make a new mold, and cast a new bell. It was brilliant in its clear tone, especially compared to the cracked bell that he had brought to me. I completed it, an exact replica, but with a tone that the ladies of the opera would envy. It was ready a week before the captain was scheduled to return.

However, the captain did not return. Other ships would come in and out of port, and I would inquire about the captain of the *Triomphant*. No one knew anything about the ship or its "Capitaine."
I continued in some hope, and as I waited, I began to polish the bell.

Every day, I would work on it some, rubbing out the rough exterior found on most ships' bells. Day after day, I would rub and polish until the bell showed forth with a lustrous finish that would have been suitable for the finest home in France.

The captain finally returned more than a year later. He regaled me with stories of his travels. I longed to be with him and his crew, so I never asked him to explain his long absence.

Finally, I presented him with the bell. He marveled at its beauty, as I hoped he would. I told him that I wanted to make a gift to him of this bell, and hoped for a small favor in return. I asked him to take me to sea, away from the fire and the blast.

The captain considered my words as his hand rubbed the bell. I could feel his appreciation for its beauty, and assumed that it had earned me my reward. His thoughtful reply stung me:

'You are not meant for the sea. There is not a man now or ever who has crossed any one of the seven seas that could make a bell so beautiful. I am not sure where your talent will lead you, but I know that if I take you to sea, you will be far from your destiny.'

He left me, saying he was off to procure the finest cheese in all of France. On his return, he sent me to you. He handed me a piece of paper, which read:

In Douai, you will find a woman named Jacqueline in her flower shop. She may help to bring you closer to your destiny.'

That is how Paul the bell founder came to me. When I told him of our bells, his eyes filled with tears, but I could not tell if they were tears of hope, despair or joy. He only said that destiny could be a cruel trickster. After saying this, he left me.

The next day, the man that the captain had sent was out in the very spot where the cannons lay. When anyone came near, he sent them away. There was banging and clanging and fire. Wagons arrived at our village, sent by Captain Laurent, with clay, bricks and wax. For months, Paul worked in solitude, coming into the village in silence for food and such. He toiled through three seasons in secret. Then, on a certain day he came to me.

'Madame, I bid you adieu,' he said, trying hard to hide his foreign tongue.

'Where will you go?' I asked. 'What mysteries have you been conjuring up in the fields all of these months?'

His silence was pained and thoughtful as he continued: 'The captain who sent me here spoke of my destiny. He knew more than he thought.
The captain knew that I am a man who can cast ships' items…including bells. He sent me here to make your bells again. I have done this. You will find them where the cannons once stood. The men of your village will need to wagon them to the steps of the town hall.'

'How did you know where to find the cannons, and how did you know what to do?' I asked. 'The bells have been long gone from the tower.'

Paul responded with deep humility: 'I believe that the captain saw the shame that I have been carrying in my heart. I somehow believe that he knew that I sought the ocean as a place to hide from myself. He has given me the gift of redemption. I will go to him now in gratitude, and ask that he take me to sea with him.'

'Redemption? Gratitude? Destiny?' I said, not knowing how to express my puzzled feelings. 'Jacqueline,' he said, 'our destinies and the fortunes of others are woven together in ways that we might never fully understand. You see, Madame, I made a bell for the captain as a way to hide from my shame. I wanted him to help me to hide on the seas. The captain saw a man that could make bells, and a woman whose destiny is to bring them back to her village. He told me of your destiny.

What he could not have known was this: As a young soldier, at the command of my home country, I helped take the bells from your village. It has caused me great shame from that day to this one.'

At this, he turned to leave. I could not believe it! I said to him, 'Sir, surely you want to enjoy the fruits of your labor. You must be here when the bells play for the very first time.'

By his response, I was surprised that he had never considered this. At first, he only wanted to leave. It was when I said, 'We need you to be here, Paul. We all do. The bells do.' "

Destiny was hard at work again. Jacqueline had no idea how much Paul would be needed.

Marc and Jacques in St. Amand...

Jacques finished playing the carillon, and was pleased to see Marc standing next to him. Having heard a few stories about Marc's behavior in the town, he was more relieved than anything. When people behave poorly, every town is a haven for gossip.

They exchanged hugs, and Marc quickly launched into his story about Estelle. He told Jacques what he had learned:

"I now know that we cannot wait for our wishes to come true. It is up to us to realize our destiny. I know now what I need to do, Jacques. I will stay here for all my days. One day, I will follow you as the carillonneur of St. Amand."

Jacques' response stung Marc:

"Destinies, son, are often realized by our own courage, this is true. But, destiny is also like the wind. It comes and it silently goes, taking some things with it while others stay. Does the seed decide its own destiny when the winds carry it days away and plant it in new soil? Does the seed decide to grow there? Can it decide to be an oak and not a chestnut? Destiny is realized not only in the journey but also in the destination.

Sometimes, I believe that the most we can do is obey the wind, enjoy the journey, and make the most of our destination. I cannot begin to guess why we end up where we do. Some of it is out of our hands, and some is mystery."

Marc listened dutifully and curiously.

Jacques continued: "The people of the town have decided, and I have agreed, that Gaston will be the one to succeed me, hopefully in many, many years." Jacques paused before continuing.

"When you chose to strangle Gaston's father as he tried to give you comfort, it gave him the leverage he needed to put his son in the place that seemingly belonged to you."

"But I didn't know!" Marc protested.

"Does that matter?"

"And you did not defend me?"

"How could I? Where were you, Marc? Did I know? Were you here to defend yourself?"

The anger which Marc thought had left him came quickly back. With it came despair, loss, and grief. Marc was fighting the feeling that had caused him to end up face down and drunk in the forest.

He was struggling to pull himself out of his depression. Every negative image from his entire life was colliding with the vision in his memory.

Jacques watched him stand. Marc's entire body strained for composure. To keep his balance, Marc extended his arm to the bench where Jacques would sit to play. He knew now that the position he had dreamed of would never be his own.

Taking in a breath that seemed it could fill the lungs of three men, and then closing his eyes momentarily, it appeared as though Marc were praying. For thirty seconds he stood there, until he swung his legs around and seated himself into playing position on the bench. He looked over at Jacques, who made no sign or sound.

His hands found the keys and the most fragile sound responded: a simple melody, such as children sing. It repeated itself like a canon before morphing seamlessly into a song that could only emanate from the heart of a man in love.

The people in the streets began to notice.
Many stopped just to listen. Couples drew themselves closer together unexpectedly.
Others thought of those that they loved and others recalled those that they had loved and lost.

As more stopped to listen and gaze upwards, a brief interlude signaled a change and the bells began to mourn woefully. Below, eyes became moist, and dormant memories of those that had been lost were rekindled. Even more people stopped to listen.

When the mourning was complete, it was as if thunder rolled with immediacy into the town. The largest of the bells sounded again and yet again, ringing in harmony to a triumphant song, like a song that is a hymn embedded into a march.

More and more of the bells joined the chorus. Not a person within the sound of the bells was able to be still.

All around St. Amand, people were popping their heads out of their windows and doors to listen.

Marc was alive and living with the bells. His playing encouraged some notes and demanded others. His body moved with great precision, yet with the appearance of wings possessed by the wind.

The music seemed to lift the bells from the tower and into heaven itself. Jacques stood nearby, his arm around his wife, who had heard the call of the bells. Both of them were aware that they were hearing that which they had never heard before, or were ever likely to hear again.

As the music crescendoed, the people prepared to applaud, but the music found an even greater height. Marc was delirious in his joy, his heart pumping in his chest and his face bathed in sweat. Five long and eerily incongruous notes ended the piece.

Before Marc's head and arms had collapsed onto the keys, a roar came from every part of the city that was generally reserved for a victory of battle.

Then it was quiet. So many hoped that the bells would begin again.

"Is it not clear that my destiny is to play the bells of St. Amand, Jacques?"

"Is St. Amand your home, Marc?"

This question cut into Marc. He noticed that he had lost the desperate feeling from before. He felt, at that moment, that he had earned the right to be claimed, and that someone should grab him and tell him: "This is your destiny and *this* is where you must stay!" He wanted to feel connected, wanted and loved. At that moment, he missed his father and felt the need to go to him.

When he told this to Jacques, his only response was, "Finally!"

They stood there, the three of them: Jacques, Françoise and Marc, holding each other, crying, and saying a wordless goodbye.

As he stood at the top step about to descend, Marc looked at his mentor for the last time. As they stood there, they were aware of the gentle wind that came through the bell tower, blowing an inviting warm wind toward the Northwest.

Marc was gone from St.Amand-Les-Eaux by nightfall. With nowhere else to go, he decided that it was time that he visited the grave of his father. It was time, indeed.

At the square in Douai...

"Why is it that I believe?" Jacqueline asked.

Before she could continue, a man interrupted her:

"Have we all forgotten the ancient story that has been passed down to us? The story about how the walls of our town teamed with the bells and with nature itself to keep us safe from invaders?"

A few sounds that signaled recognition were heard. Some of the townspeople looked quizzical, trying to remember.

"Long ago, the people of Douai felt secure in the knowledge that the walls of our town would keep us safe. They always had. Once, barbarians came and tried to scale the walls. They could not. The brave men of Douai kept them at bay.

Many of those who came to overtake us simply gave up because of the formidable walls of our town. There were far easier places for them to conquer. One particular army was only incensed by their initial defeat.

To our surprise, they camped for days outside the walls. They were so quiet that it kept the people of our town feeling uneasy, knowing that the soldiers calmly remained outside of Douai. They seemed to do nothing. In a few weeks, a large battering ram arrived. The people of Douai knew of this when they heard the barbarians' cheer at its arrival, and our spies brought back the report to the people of the town. Our townspeople could only prepare for the inevitable destruction of our ancient walls.

The invaders began at dawn. The men pushed the huge device into the wall, time after time. The wall was unyielding. It was a day of brutal cold. The skies were completely gray and without sun.

Hundreds of men grunted as they smashed the battering ram into the wall over and over again. The wall would not yield. The village spies on the wall understood the command of the leader of the invaders: they would have success by noon or leave for a weaker enemy.

Inside the walls, the people watched, and to their horror they could see cracks begin to appear and then widen slightly with each successive hit. There were still more than one and one-half hours until noon, which was when the soldiers had promised to succeed or quit their efforts: one and one-half hours until life or death.

It was approaching eleven and we were becoming more fearful. A young boy ran to the tower and up the steps, where the carillonneur was preparing to signal the bells of alarm.

Instead, the bells began to ring the noon hour strike. Many of the people, knowing full well that it was not time for the noon bells, wondered what was happening. On and on they rang: one, and then another stroke of the hour. By the sixth ring, we began to understand that the young boy had told the carillonneur to ring the noon bells early, for the sun could not argue as it hid behind the gray clouds.

The sounds of the attackers began to fade. By the strike of nine, it was nearly silent. As the largest bell rang twelve times, the order for retreat went out to the soldiers. The people of our town held their hurrahs until the barbarians were out of hearing range. Then, their cheers went up with one great voice.

The forces of nature, a young boy, and the bells had tricked a savage enemy. The people of Douai blessed them all on that day."

The funeral…

A middle-aged man stepped forward, anxious to tell his story of the bells. He began in this way:

"The bells once rang for us, calling us to work and to worship. Sometimes, it seemed as though they were our voice. I have felt great sadness that the bells will not call out when I finally leave this earth.

When I was a boy, I recall how the funeral wagon would wind down from the hills and move slowly through the town on the way to the cemetery. When my youngest son died, I walked with the rest of my family in slow procession behind the wagon that carried him.

I cannot describe my sadness completely enough. In a matter-of-fact manner, my wife delivered the news that our son had died. I was surprised that she was not sadder than she was.

As the wagon led us to the graveyard, the bells were pounding a dirge into our hearts. They rang with sadness.

I noticed that my wife's cries, the cries of a mother, had begun softly. They soon became louder and louder, and each cry mimicked the note of a bell. It was as if the bells were teaching her the sad song to sing...helping her to loose the sorrow from her heart.

When the song was over, the largest bell tolled eight times...one for each year of a short life."

Jacqueline talks to the townspeople a few days before Christmas...

"Which is it, do you suppose?" Jacqueline asked of everyone and no one. "Were the bells made for us, or were we made for the bells?

Some felt that when the foreigners took our bells, they took our lives. Do you recall how they lowered the bells into the wagons that stood at this very spot, as they grunted all the while? Do you remember how the smaller of the bells were thrown cruelly onto the courtyard where we now stand, to shatter without mercy? Do you remember how our hearts were torn from the inside of us?"

A man of the village, known for his love of wine, took the attention from Jacqueline:

"You are an old fool, Jacqueline, a dreamer! A dreamer who tries to make us all believe that there is some golden magic in those bells! The bells were of another time. Yet, you cannot let it rest. You charm the foolish people of the village with this nonsense of long ago. Now here they all stand: a bunch of fools that have been led happily to nowhere."

Some of those assembled seemed to agree, while some mumbled agreement. A young man, perhaps of twenty-five, came forward. His hands were thrust deeply into his pockets and the look on his face was defiant.

"With all due respect, Madame, I must agree. You have made fools of my family and me. We came here today for magic. There is no magic that I can see, but you did succeed in tricking me into sweating and heaving the bells into the tower. And for what? You remind me of my foolish old grandfather who talks as if the taking of the bells from Douai was equal in history to the flood that covered the world. For my entire life, I have heard about the bells that no longer exist, as if they were ghosts. I have lived here all of my twenty-five years and I have no need for any bells. I am a happy farmer. Please, now that you have your infernal bells back in the tower, can we not just live in peace? If I never hear about the bells again, it will be too soon."

Turning to those assembled, sweeping his arm across the square, he addressed them all:

"Let the folklore of the bells die away with our ancestors. *Our* generation must lead our village forward."

"You are a young man of the village," Jacqueline responded. "I understand the bells are like an ancient rhyme to you. But, this you must know: I, too, have cursed and reviled these bells, much like we sometimes do to our own families. There have been many days when I wished that they would stop calling to me, but they do not. Perhaps the bells will never play again. Perhaps your generation will never hear them as we have in the past. But, I encourage you to know this: *the bells* will decide if they will be silenced, not *your* generation."

"My fear, old woman, is that you truly believe this."

This did not insult Jacqueline, although the tension could be felt all around her.

"Have you ever traveled to another village, son?"

"Of course!"

"And when they ask where you are from, what do you tell them?"

"I say 'Douai', of course. Do you think that I cannot name my own home?"

"And what do they ask when you tell them where you are from?"

The silence answered the question for everyone assembled. "They ask about the bells…"

Marc arrives in Douai to visit the grave of his father…

Marc entered the town in the midst of it all. He had made a long journey to get to Douai. As he arrived, he was still a little uncertain as to why he had come. Still, he knew that he was responding to something… it was as if he had been summoned there.

He had been here once before…fifteen years ago. He had come to bury his father. And, when he had come, he did not remain for even a full day. Now that he had come to visit him again, he hoped for direction. Still, he did not feel as though he had been traveling without a purpose.

There was so little that he knew. Would his life have been different had he known more? Would he have made this journey?

All that he knew of his mother was what his father had told him: she had died before his first birthday from a sickness that was never named. He had learned quite early that his father found any conversation or questions about his mother to be painful.

Things unknown to Marc...

Marc did not know that his father, aged nineteen at the time, had spent five years as an apprentice to Vincent, the town carillonneur. Behind his back, the people of the town called Vincent "the Maestro" in a fashion that was not complimentary. In some ways, Henri had been like a personal attendant to Vincent. He was expected to fetch his tea and his wine and to market for him.

When Vincent played the bells, Marc's father, Henri, was to stand at attention, behind the Maestro.
He was expected to pay strict attention and to never, ever crowd Vincent while he played. If he did, he would be shoved away by one of the carillonneur's long and gangly arms, as they circled about to pound the next note of the bells.

The Maestro would often turn his head to be sure that Henri was studying each of his moves, and if he sensed any lack of concentration, Henri would receive a shove as the Maestro would shout, "Attention! Watch me and learn! Feel the joy of the bells!"

But, the way that the Maestro said this did not seem as though *he* was feeling joy.

What the Maestro seemed to love more than the bells was the position they gave him in the community, and the fact that it provided him with his own personal attendant.

But, Henri endured it all because he loved the bells. His earliest memories as a young boy of the village were the sounds of the bells as they cascaded over his head, as he would wander about the gardens of the manor that was his home.

Henri could remember days when he and his father would go by coach to the town square, where his father would conduct business. Henri called out with delight when he discovered the mysterious spot where the bells lived atop the tower at town hall. He wished he could touch them, but also loved them for their cloistered mystery.

Henri's father, the Count, would take Henri on his rounds and business about town. But, when the bells were playing, Henri would often stop just to listen, which always caused his father to reprimand Henri: "Keep up!" Sometimes, his father would call him a daydreamer, but always with a smile on his face.

The Count seemed to know that the bells called more loudly to some than to others. Sometimes, he would stop and listen also, with a relaxed smile on his face that quickly vanished as he returned to the thoughts of his appointments.

It was the Count who suggested to Vincent that he take Henri as an apprentice, with the explanation that his son heard music, while others heard only the sound of bells.

Henri began to study the carillon with the Maestro by the time that he was fourteen years old.
Even though he lived a life of leisure and luxury, there was no time he enjoyed more, regardless of the pompous way the Maestro treated him.

Henri's way to deal with the cruelty of his teacher was to envision the day that the old man died and the seat in the tower would be his and his alone.

In the first five years that Henri had apprenticed, he had played the actual bells only once. On his seventeen[th] birthday, after many requests to have the chance to play, the Maestro finally acquiesced.
As Henri sat down on the bench, his emotions were torn between timidity, exhilaration, and fear as he felt the Maestro's presence over him.

At first, he struck the keys in a respectful, almost frightened way. He had chosen to play a piece that he had watched the Maestro perform many times. As Henri played the notes timidly, but correctly, the Maestro roared at him: "Play the *instrument*! Do *not* let it play *you*!" and, "Take command!"

Henri was completely unaware of the words that were being screamed at him. He *was* allowing the bells to play him. It was as if he were touching and caressing the lover he had longed for.

The music washed over him in waves until he was no longer playing the bells. He had *become* the music of the bells. He could see and feel himself floating above the town and across the fields. He rode the notes as if they were the wind.

He saw himself look down on his father as he relaxed in the gardens of the manor, and saw his father look up as the music passed over him with the smile that only the bells could bring to his face.

Henri was inspired in his playing. All of those who heard it that day knew that the notes, although the same as always, *felt* very different.

When the Maestro finally pounded on Henri's shoulders enough to remove him from his trance-like state with the bells, he did so with the words, "You play as a fool!" But the words had no effect on Henri because he knew the truth, and he knew the Maestro did, also. The Maestro treated the bells in the same manner that he treated Henri: as a servant or slave. But, Henri and the bells had become one.

Later that day, the Maestro walked across the square with Henri, his attendant, walking dutifully behind him. Several of the townspeople, assuming it was he who had played so beautifully, stopped the Maestro to ask why he had stopped the piece in the middle. This incident was never spoken of between the teacher and the student again.

Henri knew that there was no point in asking to play again in the near future. He knew that all he could do was wait. He was ashamed that sometimes he wished that the Maestro would die.

Sometimes, the people of the town noticed that Henri had taken to "playing" the bells as he sat under a tree, or even when he walked about. His arms circled and struck and sometimes pounded the carillon that was so real in his imagination.

Many of the people of the town of Douai knew these facts well. Yet, all were unknown to Marc.

Two days before Christmas...

At first, Marc was quizzical. He had followed the sounds from the hill. It had been like a steady buzzing all of the way, but when he reached the town square everyone was quiet and seemed to be fixated upon one woman. It was clear that they were waiting for her to speak and just as clear to Marc that she did not know what to say. The look on her face seemed to reflect patience and curiosity, as if she were waiting for direction or inspiration.
When she finally spoke, it was in a voice that seemed familiar to him, but he knew, of course, it could not have been. She spoke with great command and with even greater wisdom:

"Have we learned *nothing?*"

When she asked the question, all eyes were upon her.

Someone said, in a voice meant to be heard, but quiet enough to conceal the identity of the speaker, "Yes, we have learned that we are fools and dreamers. What will we do next, build a fishing dock on the hillside and expect fish?" A few laughed softly.

Jacqueline let the comment pass, and then spoke again:

"Have we not learned that what we need will come to us, if only we believe? Didn't we have the noon bells that tricked our enemies, and a mysterious man who cast our bells to save his own soul?"

Marc was taking in every word while watching the faces of the townspeople, and absorbing the view of the town. He saw the shops and the fountain. He saw the hills roll away from the square. He saw the expert way in which the town square had been neatly cobbled. Where it was not covered by the townspeople, he noticed the white stone of the steps that led up to the façade of the impressive town hall. It was as if he knew what he would see before his eyes took it in.

Slowly, it came back to Marc. He had been to this town fifteen years before. He had come here to bury his father and had left quickly.

He ambled about for many years, hoping to find a destination. He could not have known that he had found his destination long ago, because it had not been the right time.

Now, it seemed that time and places and events had all come together to bring him here again.
Only now, he was not thinking about leaving. For a man who had been something of a rootless gypsy for a long time, he finally had a feeling of home.

He began walking around the townspeople, inching along toward the front, not wanting to miss a single word that the woman was saying. He was drawn to her.

"We have worked so hard and endured so very much to have our pride back in our town. Surely, the word will go out and someone will appear. If the word does not do so, then the wind will cry out, and if necessary, *the bells themselves* will call their master to them. The bells will not always be silent. Indeed, they will not always be silent. Let us hope and pray that the word goes out from our town, and that we welcome the one who will play our bells."

A derisive voice filled with boldness and arrogance said, "Hasn't the word gone out already? Didn't we say that the Christmas season would draw from far and wide and the bells would play as they used to? Haven't we had people here all day from many different places, many of whom are with us still? Why are we still assembled here? Perhaps there is no one who can or wishes to play our bells."

Marc seemed to hear the words before all of the rest of them. It was as if they were spoken *to him*, for the rest of the folks to hear.

When he spoke, it was with a voice that was new to him:

"*I* can play the bells."

There was murmuring among the people until someone asked of all present, "What did he say?"

Marc answered for himself, "I can play the bells!" As he did, his arms moved in the rhythmic, sweeping gestures of a carillonneur. He struck five imaginary keys, singing their notes as he did so, "bum, bum, bum, bum, bum…"

The reaction of those gathered was oddly mixed. Some felt relief, others surprise, and still others joy. Some felt certainty, and some disbelief. Marc felt nothing on his own, but could sense all of these feelings around him.

Mostly, he just exchanged fixed stares with the woman, whose face fully concealed whatever she was feeling.

"Tell us! Tell us! Where have you played, and who was your teacher? Tell us! Why have you sought to come to our town…to play our bells?"

As Marc began to speak, the townspeople began to circle around him.

"Just moments ago, when I arrived in your town square, I began to feel that I had come home…home to a place that lived only in distant dreams and stories.

My father raised me in the town of Dunkerque. We lived there, he and I, for all of my youth. When we woke in the morning, we would walk to a tiny carpentry shop near the docks. We would work from the sunrise to the sunset, to fill the homes of the rich with fine furniture. As a boy, I sat by his side. As I grew older, I began to help him. As my father became weaker, it was I who worked with the wood while he sat by my side.

He seldom spoke. I knew little of him other than his devotion to me and to the bells that rang in his memory. As we went through our work during the day, he was quiet and distracted. It always seemed as though his heart and mind were somewhere else.

At night, we played the bells. First he, then he and I, and then only I played the bells. When he played, he seemed so alive and content."

"What bells?" the people of the town asked, as if with one voice. "Where were the bells that he played?"

Someone hollered, "He is a liar and a fool! There are no bells in Dunkerque. It is a village by the sea."

There were some jeers and some laughter, and a few people began to walk away.

"Tell us about these bells!" the woman said, in a voice that commanded all of their attention and brought them to silence.

Marc smiled at the woman. *She knows more than the rest*, he thought to himself. He would tell her. The rest could laugh all that they wanted. He knew that he was telling the story of his life.

He knew that many destinies make magic. His story was a small but important piece of something greater than himself.

And so, Marc continues...

"We shared a tiny room, my father and I. Two cots were all we had until he built what he called the carillonneur's bench."

A few chuckled when someone asked sarcastically, "A phantom bench for the imaginary bells?"

"He would sit at the bench and play, like this:"

Marc seated himself on the steps of the town hall. His arms moved slowly and gracefully, striking the bells of his imagination. "Bum, bum, bum, bum, bum"... his voice marked sharply the five distinct notes. It was not at all unlike the pealing of the bells.

"Sometimes, he would sit for hours, playing the music that was in his head. As soon as I was able, he began to teach me, like this:"

Marc sang the five notes, the fifth being decidedly sour. At this point, he swung an imaginary pointer as if to strike the head of someone seated at the bench. "My father would say in a loud voice, 'No! No!' whenever I placed my hands in the wrong position."

Another voice, rich in sarcasm asked, "Who are you, then? Are you the *spirit* of the bells?"

"Did you know the Maestro?" another asked.

"Not at all," Marc replied.

A voice bellowed, "So, you never knew the Maestro, *and* your father played the bells in a village without bells, *and* he taught you in your bedroom! *This* is how you claim to know the bells?"

"Yes. And, in St. Amand, I continued to learn the carillon, and much of life, from Jacques Lannoy."

The shock of hearing the name of the most famous carillonneur in all of France made the crowd gasp to an uncomfortable silence. Still, Marc knew words would not be enough to convince them.

His legs climbed the steps to the tower, two at a time. Finally, he felt that time and place were put together for him to seize and to make his own.

He slid onto the bench, his hands and feet immediately at work, commanding the bells into song. There was no gentle introduction. The bells were in full song from the very start. They rang as if they were announcing themselves to the heavens and the hills. They did so with a song that would have been familiar to anyone who was in the square in Douai thirty years ago.

People tipped their heads to listen. You could see the recognition on their faces, as if they knew what the next note would be. They smiled the smile of someone watching a friend return home after a long absence.

The bells were playing again, indeed. The music was invigorating the people of Douai, reaching up to the stars and pouring into their hearts. The square was joyful and filled with happy mayhem.

Jacqueline stood alone in one place. She had become as a statue, her head tilted toward the music. Her hands were clasped, resting upon her heart. When he finished the song, Marc returned quickly to the square. Jacqueline approached him slowly.

"Who are you, young man?"

"I am Marc."
"How is it that you know that song?"

"My father always used to hum that song when I was a young boy."

"And your father's name?"

"Henri."

When she heard the name "Henri", Jacqueline could feel her heart racing. She chose her next words very carefully:

"Your father told you of Douai, and how it was here that he learned the bells? He told you all about our town and how our bells were taken? And, that you should return here to the play the bells for us?"

"He did not. Why do you ask this of me?"

"A young man used to play that song for me many years ago. The last time I saw him, he gave me a shattered piece of bronze from our old bells that were destroyed many years ago."

Marc fumbled for a moment, until he found the small oval piece of metal that he wore on a leather strap around his neck, under his shirt. Withdrawing it, he held it in the palm of his hand, fingers encircled around it. He slowly opened his fingers, almost afraid to reveal it in his outstretched palm.

As Jacqueline stared at the piece of bronze in awe and disbelief, she collapsed…collapsed like a leaf that has surrendered the tree and yielded to the wind. Before fully melting into the hard stone of the street, a voice that keened as it came from Jacqueline exclaimed: "My heart!"

Those standing by reacted slowly to this strange display. Slowly, they made a small circle around her. One woman began to fan the fallen woman's face while she called for water.

"Is she dead?"

"No," the woman responded, without taking her eyes from Jacqueline. "Her chest heaves. Her eyelids flutter."

A man who shuffled more than he walked pushed through the circle and painfully knelt beside her.

"She screamed, 'my heart!' as she fell." The woman explained to the old man, as she continued to fan Jacqueline, "I fear that her heart is giving way."

The old man caressed Jacqueline's hair. "Not at all," he said, "Not at all. I am her father. The song that he played was the song that her lover played for her long ago, in this same place, in the same way."

Slowly, Jacqueline's eyes opened. Her focus was returning. She gasped first at the sight of Marc, who was so close. She gasped louder still when she knew she was feeling the touch of her own father's hand for the first time in thirty years.

As they helped Jacqueline to stand, she could not remove her eyes from Marc.

"Please, tell me more of how you know this song."

"My father often hummed it while he worked." Marc replied. "When I asked him what it was, he would always say: 'It is the song of my heart, and hers.'"

Jacqueline looked first at her father and then at Marc.

"A young man named Henri wrote that song for me many years ago. We were very much in love, but our parents would not allow us to marry, even though I was carrying his child. He then left Douai and never returned."

Jacqueline trembled. She looked at her father. His face displayed none of the anger and shame that had kept them apart for so many years.

"My own father put me out. I went to the Convent of St. Anne and gave birth to our child. I was forced to leave the child in the Sisters' care at the orphanage. I was a frightened young girl, and I was alone. The piece of bell that you carry was all that your father had to give you. I was the one who left it with you. You are my son. I am your mother."

No further words were needed.

The people react to the icon from the old bells...

Jacqueline was vibrant. Happiness had restored her strength. Standing with her son, she said to the people that were gathered:

"Do you remember? Have you forgotten the magic of the bells?"

There was a silence, then murmuring and then, the low rumble of indistinct voices. Words were being exchanged as the looks on the faces of the people of Douai were changing from surprise to the broad grins of a people that are truly jubilant.

"I have had mine since the day the bells were shattered."

"Mine is from my father."

"We found this one tied to my sister's bible, in a small sack."

"I have carried mine in my pocket every day, from then until now. I thought that I was the only one!"

They extended one arm into the air, each one of them. Each was holding a piece of a bell from long ago.

Secrets are hard to keep. However, to keep a secret that covers an entire community for over thirty years is seemingly impossible.

It seemed as though every hand in Douai was now lifted up, holding their seemingly insignificant piece of bell. They were all so busy noticing that every person shared the same secret, that they were completely unaware of the obvious. All, that is, except Paul.

Paul, the bell founder, was generally a quiet, thoughtful man. Even in the midst of all the accusations and the threats on his life, he had remained fairly calm and reasonable. He was now jumping up and down like a man that had suddenly been infested by demons. It took a while before they understood the words he was screaming:

"There is your bell! There is your missing bell! You have all kept it from me, and accused *me*!"

Paul tore the hat from his head and began collecting the pieces from them. He did not need to insist. They all gave them willingly. Soon, the hat was nearly overflowing, so a merchant brought a large basket to him. When Paul poured the collected bits, which must have come from many different bells, they collided into each other in a series of notes, rather than the expected dissonant clanging of metal.

When all, save one, had made their contribution, Marc approached the bell founder. He dropped his bit of bronze, along with its leather strap, amongst the rest of them.

Paul placed the basket, now of a considerable weight, onto the ground. He picked up Marc's shard and held it in his hand. Paul looked first at Marc and then into the faces of those close by.

"Surely, with all that Marc has lost, you will want him to keep this memento of his father."

Marc replied without delay or hesitation. "My father would give this up willingly, as do I. Without it, the carillon remains incomplete."

Jacqueline smiled the faint sort of smile that often accompanies tears.

"When I asked my father about my mother, a look of grief that was so profound crossed his face. I learned that the memory of her was so dear and tragic that he could not endure to remember her. It is all that I know of love. He guarded this icon until he died."

"Died?"

"Yes. I brought him here, to the place that he called home, fifteen years ago, and buried him on the hill with the paupers."

Jacqueline gasped slightly at the mention of the word "paupers".

He ignored her and continued:

"My life has been a quiet mystery to me in many ways. I was raised by the most silent of men who filled my head with music and my heart with bells. He gave me no home, so my feet were made to wander.

In my mind, I have been searching for a home…a home where the bells beckoned to me. But, it is not the bells alone that called me to this place, is it?"

The question hung heavy in the air for them all. The only sound to be heard was Paul. He grunted his way over the hill, struggling with a particularly noisy basket of metal.

Jacqueline speaks...

"I have lived a life of hope and misery. It seemed to me that the things that were sent to me for love or pleasure were given to me so briefly, that it was only in losing them that I knew them at all. Still, I have tried to live with a sense of hope. The symbol of my hope was the bells of this town. I thought that the bells called to me and it was in their ringing that my heart would be restored. I had hoped that my love would come back to me in them: my love that lived in the manor, who now lies with the paupers.

In my life, I have wondered these things, more than all others:

-Are we meant to discover whom we were meant to be?

Or

-Are we meant to dream, and to create that which we want to be?

This much I know: whichever we choose, we will need to have faith, we will need to believe in others and we will need courage. But, there is so much that I never knew. I never knew...I never knew that my son would find his way to me by listening to the bells."

As Marc and his mother embraced, the entire town made a hurrah, as if with one voice.

Marc then returned to the tower to play for the people.

The bells had returned to Douai. They would play for Christmas.

A reunion...

Marc had little to say. He was, it seemed, overcome by it all. When everyone else had left the square that night, Jacqueline took his arm and together they walked to her home in silence. On a cot above the flower shop, he slept immediately and deeply. For the first night in many, he was dreamless.

His eyes opened the next morning, slowly focusing on a mug of tea and a slice of coarse bread waiting for him. He rose slowly and smiled. His mind was filled with so many things to tell and to ask that he had no idea where to begin.

After some moments, he found a washbowl and filled it with water from the pitcher. He then splashed some onto his face, waking slowly. He walked to the window and looked out at the rising sun. In the square below, he could see his mother arranging various flowers into small bouquets, which she knotted with a rough twine.

As he watched her, he had a growing sense that he had no idea of how to greet her, or how she might greet him. He was trying to put together what he might say to her. When he saw her holding a bunch of flowers in her hand, it gave him the answer.

When he came to her on the square, she was sitting behind the cart on the bench that he knew so well.

Marc extended one hand to her wordlessly while he took a bunch of flowers in the other.

"Come with me?" he asked.

She came to her feet immediately, her hand remaining in his. They walked from the square slowly, neither saying very much at first.

"Tell me, where did you get that bench?"

Of all the questions that he might ask, this one was a surprise to Jacqueline.

"I bought it from a woman in Douai long ago. Why?"

"It is the bench that Papa made to teach me the carillon. I left it at his grave on the day I buried him. He would be pleased that you have it."

In light of all that happened in the last days, Jacqueline accepted this additional mysterious coincidence without the need to question it.

Jacqueline and Marc arrived at Henri's grave, poorly marked nearly fifteen years ago in the paupers' field. They were both aware that this was the closest that they would ever come to being together as a family. They then placed the flowers on Henri's grave.

They spent the afternoon and the evening together, talking of all that had happened. It was now Christmas Eve.

In Douai at Christmas, the bells will carol...

Every year, the town had a Christmas celebration that lasted throughout the twelve days of Christmas.

Paul had toiled to make the final bell and Jacqueline was pleased to find it outside of her door when she awoke on the morning of Christmas Eve.
Volunteers were easily found to put it in place.
Only Jacqueline seemed to notice that Paul was gone. Recalling their earlier conversation, she was certain that his destiny was now fully realized.

With the final bell in place, and with the feeling that Christmas brings, Jacqueline was completely taken up with all of the joy that surrounded her. She was jubilant and had a youthful aura about her. She told one person after another that they should never believe that happiness was not meant for them.

"Look at me!" she would say. "In just these few days, I have found that my true love rests right here in our village. I have found a son that I believed was lost to me forever. And, of course, the bells will carol for us all in just one more hour."

Marc smiled when he would hear her tell this story over and over. He would watch from a few paces away as she received and returned warm hugs of gratitude and congratulation. He thought to himself, *this is truly her day.*

As Jacqueline moved about the square recounting her story and accepting the good wishes of the townspeople, she was sure to wish everyone "Merry Christmas!"

And, just to be sure of her good fortune, she would often turn just to gaze at Marc, who had not moved very far from his spot in front of the tower steps.

She felt a sense of terror when she noticed that Marc was flanked on either side by her parents, Christine and Pierre. Her first reaction was to keep her father from him, but the truth was that she was too afraid.

Her father was talking to Marc now, quite loudly, with his arms moving in an exaggerated fashion. Jacqueline inched closer, hoping that courage would come to her. She stopped when she heard her father saying:

"I was standing right over there, and your *grand-mere* was over there, with a bunch of tomatoes in her apron. The bells were playing and we were both looking up…"

Jacqueline saw her father affectionately place his hand on Marc's shoulder. She saw Marc smiling. And she could not help but smile herself.

For on this Christmas, there would be singing and gifts and praise and gratitude and triumph and bells… **The Bells.**

~

Author's Note

The fourth book by d.ennis is not a work entirely of his own imagination. It is based on a concept by Frank Della Penna.

The author wishes to thank Frank for the opportunity to tell a story of hope, conviction, and miracles.

This book is the basis for a new theatrical production being created by Cast In Bronze called "The Bells." The musical will feature the carillon on stage for the very first time in history. Cast In Bronze hopes to bring "The Bells" to audiences across America so they can discover the beauty and majesty of the carillon for themselves.

    For more information about Cast In Bronze or to obtain the CD from the musical "The Bells," please visit:

www.castinbronze.com

For more information on the author, please visit:

www.denniscoleman.net

About Frank DellaPenna

I have spoken to enough fans of Frank DellaPenna and Cast In Bronze, to know how eager you are to know more about the "man of mystery."

I certainly wouldn't want to be the one to divulge what Frank looks like, because he has worked so hard to guard that secret.
I can tell you, however, that on the "handsome scale" that Frank is about halfway between Ron Howard and Johnny Depp.

There are some things, however, that I am happy to tell you about Frank.

I have known him since elementary school, which was quite a while ago. At that time, we lived a mile apart in a rural section of Chester County in Pennsylvania. We were little league teammates and graduated from high school together.

After high school, we took divergent paths. Frank went off to college with hopes of becoming a health and physical education teacher. Luckily for his fans, those plans changed.

Shortly after college, Frank married and took his beautiful bride Anne to France for several years, to complete his education on the carillon.

Both Frank and I were fortunate to come from what they now refer to as a "functional family." His parents are warm and wonderful people that always made me feel comfortable in their home.

I can recall vividly how I made Frank play the piano for me when we were at his house. I was as amazed at his abilities when we were ten years old, as I am today.

You would be interested to know that Frank was an athlete of the highest standards in high school; excelling in both football and wrestling. He was the only kid that I knew that received acclaim for both his sporting accomplishments as well as his musical talents. In school, Frank was popular and fun, but more importantly, he was, to quote a mutual friend, "always a gentleman." He remains one.

Today, Frank and I again live within a few miles of each other, in rural Chester County, fifteen miles from where we grew up. In between our childhood days and the present, there were often long spaces where we did not see each other, outside of the occasional high school reunion.

As mentioned, Frank lived for some years in France. He also lived in Maryland for several years during the time that he sold the sort of bells that he plays today. He also worked in the contracting business and all the while, he would play the carillon at various cathedrals. Even during our long periods apart, Frank was often on my mind.

The biography that I most want to share is this one. I worked for many years as a youth worker, for high school kids. Many of the discussions that I had with the kids were about making the right choices, in what is often a tumultuous time of life.

Frank DellaPenna often served as a model for living, and when I told his story, I always described him as having a moral compass that always-pointed North.

I would describe him in ways that the kids could relate to. As a great athlete, a good scholar, good-looking, a great musician, a good friend and a guy that was popular with everyone, including teachers, and still "cool."

When I would ask the kids to think of the one or two classmates that seemed to have everything going for them, they could always name them. They would often describe them as being detached, or condescending, and often they were seen as downright hurtful.

Frank had none of those attributes. He was fair minded and kind to everyone. Rather than being a physical or emotional bully, Frank was the guy that would protect the kids that needed it.

I don't want to paint a picture of Frank that makes him appear as a goody-goody, because he was not. He enjoyed fun and mischief nearly as much as I did. Frank knew where the boundaries were and he didn't cross them. Doing the right thing was never a struggle for Frank.

There are some boundaries that Frank does not recognize however, and that is how his music, and this book, came into existence.

Consider this to start. Frank plays an instrument that very few people understand, and most have never even seen, given the fact that the Carillon resides in a bell tower.

To say that Frank loves the Carillon would be to understate it. He maintains a great desire to share this exotic instrument with the world.
This is no easy feat when the instrument weighs eight thousand pounds. This was only a minor inconvenience to him. I can guess that he was surprised, but I am certain that he was grateful, when, through providence, a man delivered to Frank the only traveling Carillon in the U.S. His hope was that Frank would bring it to the people, and he has.

The magic of having a bell tower put on wheels is a major accomplishment, to be sure. But that is probably incidental compared to the fact that now you need to convince people to let you play it for them. I imagine this:

"Excuse me sir, but I play an instrument that weighs four tons that you never heard of. If you can just give me forty feet or so, I would love to set it up and play for people."

Only a man that refuses to accept the boundaries that block his dreams could have persevered.

Today, Frank DellaPenna plays the Carillon ten months out of the year, hauling it, by himself, around America.

He plays beautiful compositions of his own creation as well as treating his listeners to wondrous arrangements of songs that are familiar to them.

Afterwards they line up to buy his CD's so that they can have this mysterious music in their homes.

If you are not impressed by this fact, then tell me how many other carillon records are in your collection.

Frank has indeed brought the music of the carillon to the people; his audiences have included Presidents, Popes, and rock stars.

Not long ago, Frank decided that some other boundaries needed removing and so he set himself upon the task of creating a musical presentation that tells the story that Frank wants us to know. He wants to tell his story in a way that features the carillon, along with actors and musicians and choirs.

He also decided that I would write the story for him. I tried to resist, but it was pointless.

So, I have acquiesced to the wishes of an old friend. My task was to find a way to get the message out to others that have guided Frank's improbable life. It's a simple story really. Frank believes one thought more than all others:

Find a way to live out your dreams. It's a simple matter of taking the improbable and kicking it into reality by believing equally in three things. Miracles, yourself, and other people.

How else could you roll into town with a truck full of bells, put on a black outfit and a mask, and perform music that simultaneously lifts people up and makes them cry?

About Anne DellaPenna

No dreamer ever managed to bring a dream to reality without the support of those close to them.

When Frank decided to bring the carillon to the rest of us, he needed someone to say "Sure darling, go and do that. I'll be here raising the kids and making a living."

There would be no "Cast In Bronze" without Anne. It's that simple. It is not enough that she loves her husband and believes in him. She has enabled her husband to take enormous risks, and is happy to reside far from the limelight.

I'm fairly certain that Anne would say that she has not done anything extraordinary to help Frank realize his dreams. That is the beauty of this woman.

Some of you may have seen her. She can sometimes be found buzzing around the merchandise tent where Cast In Bronze is appearing; making sure that everything is running smoothly. Following that, she will figure out wherever Frank has gotten to, and make sure that he is running smoothly.

Frank DellaPenna married a beautiful girl more than thirty years ago. The outstanding thing about Anne is that her beauty is hardly her major asset.

She is a wonderful person that has brought out the very best in a good and talented man.

Frank DellaPenna is seated at his carillon, with the author.